Chronicles of the Kilner Family

I

LEAH

WORDEXCERPT

COPYRIGHT

Chronicles of the Kilner Family
Leah

Translation by Paul W. Anderson
Edited by R.A. Piper

First published in Korea in 2018 by Shinyoung Media Service, INC.
English Translation © 2021 by WordExcerpt LLC.

Visit us at:
wordexcerpt.com
facebook.com/wordexcerpt
twitter.com/wordexcerpt
instagram.com/wordexcerpt

First Edition: September 2021

WordExcerpt is an imprint of WordExcerpt LLC. The WordExcerpt name and logo are trademarks of WordExcerpt LLC.

The publisher is not responsible for websites (or their content) that are not owned by the publisher.

ISBN 978-1-954707-03-0 (digital)
978-1-954707-22-1 (paperback)

You should have kept coming even if I told you to disappear! You should've come even if I said I never wanted to see you ever again!

One

"How's the cleaning?"

"It's nearly done."

"And what of the blanket I told you to take care of?"

"I sent that child to pick it up. They'll bring it soon."

The richest household in the village, the Kilner family buzzed with activity, undergoing a large-scale cleaning project the likes of which had not been seen by them in quite a while.

The hardest worker amongst them was Madam

Jane, the lady of the house. She had been working diligently since early morning, forgoing any breaks to ensure that everything was ready for the guests set to arrive later in the day. She strode tirelessly through every corner of the house, pointing out all the little flaws she deemed in need of correction, yet the true labor lied in the efforts of the Kilner family's hired workers, who broke their backs in attendance of every demand.

"I'm not sure if the food is being prepared properly. Have I already informed the chef that they should never put mushrooms in the soup?" Madam Jane asked Samantha.

Samantha was a woman who served as the head of all the employees. She had been a facet of the Kilner household ever since she was twelve years old, staying with them even until she grew into middle age and her hair began to show hints of grey.

She tried to coax Jane into relaxing, shrewdly crafting a reassuring response. "Yes, you did. Everything is progressing smoothly thanks to you, madam," she said. "So, why don't you leave the work to your underlings for now and relax with a cup of tea?"

"This is all for my child who's finally returning after three long years away from us, Samantha." Madam Jane tried to stifle the overwhelming joy surging through her heart, willing herself into suppressing her rising blush. She spoke with her hand atop her pounding chest. "Excitement of this magnitude won't go away with just a cup of tea and a nice, calming seat!"

She rushed toward the underground level where the house's kitchen was located.

Exasperated, Samantha began to mumble to herself. "Why don't you realize that sitting down and not doing anything would help us out far more?" she bemoaned, before hurriedly chasing down the stairs after Jane.

✳ ✳ ✳

Anna entered a room at the end of the third-floor hallway holding a winter blanket larger than herself in her arms. She placed the blanket upon the room's bare bed.

Inside of the room, cleaning it, were two women older than her. After setting the blanket down, one of the women, who had been sweeping the floor, approached Anna wordlessly and helped her spread the blanket over the bed. Anna nodded to her in gratitude, silently thanking her for the help.

The woman stopped to look toward the window. "He's here," she hastily whispered.

Anna's gaze naturally followed the exclamation and she glanced outside the window as well. There she spotted a horse carriage riding toward the house, treading upon the grassy weeds as it did so.

The woman who was helping Anna couldn't help but give into her curiosity so she approached the window fully. Anna opted to watch as well, so she settled beside her, catching the carriage just as it slowed to a stop at the front entrance of the building.

The coachman got off and opened the door of the carriage, revealing the dashing figure of a young man as he alighted from his seat. Anna could recognize at a glance that he was the second oldest young master of the Kilner family: Dylan Kilner. Dylan looked manlier and much sturdier than he did on the day he first left three years ago.

The whole family waited beside the entrance, eager to greet Dylan. Sir Crane and his wife, Madame Jane, stood beside the eldest son of the house, David, and David's wife, Carol. Dylan individually embraced them each, one after another, with the only exception being Carol, his sister-in-law, to which he provided a kiss on the back of the hand instead. It was an ordinary greeting, but it was accomplished with a sophisticated and noble air.

The last woman who was cleaning, a blonde, spoke up, chastising the two girls by the window. "If you want to lose your jobs and end up homeless on the streets, keep lazing around like that," she said.

She had been left to mop the floor alone while the other two watched the family reunion, mesmerized as they were by the Kilners' elegance.

"Especially you," the blonde continued. She rested her hand on her waist and glared, pointing a finger right at the pale woman standing next to Anna. "How could you laze around like that when you don't have a sponsor willing to bear the brunt of the consequence for you should you make a mistake?"

The pale woman lowered her head in guilt and retrieved her forgotten broom to resume sweeping. However, it was not she whom the blonde had an issue with. In truth, her qualms laid with Anna. The blonde was condemning Anna in a subtle way, indirectly insinuating that Anna had it easier than the rest of them because she had someone to fall back on in case she screwed up.

However, Anna couldn't find it in herself to react angrily at the blonde despite hearing those malicious words. She didn't like how the blonde was disparaging the individual supporting her by calling them a 'sponsor', but it was true that she was able to work in a more relaxed manner in comparison to other employees of the Kilner family thanks to them. The only thing that Anna felt was truly unfair was that she and the person behind her never wrongfully begged for forgiveness nor did they provide excuses whenever she made a mistake. With a shrug of her shoulders, Anna turned back to look outside the window once more, only to find that the house's lively and populous front yard was now completely empty.

"You look much more capable than you did three years ago, Dylan," David, Dylan's older brother, said. He smiled warmly as he lifted his wine glass.

Dylan grinned playfully, his perfect teeth peeking through. "Three years is not a short time, after all."

A clinking sound rang out as the brothers' wine

glasses lightly tapped each other. Blood red wine danced within each glass.

"You know that, so why did it take you three years to come back to us?" Madam Jane interjected. "I was worrying about you day after day, concerned about whether or not you were eating or sleeping properly. At the very least, you should have sent a letter, or—"

Sir Crane cut her off. "So you've completely returned?" he asked Dylan. Jane glared at her husband for the intrusion.

"Yes, I've completely returned," Dylan nodded.

Hearing this, Madam Jane shed a tear of genuine happiness. Sir Crane scolded her display of emotion, citing that she was making a fool of herself, but his claims were tempered by the way he held her hand and took a handkerchief from his pocket, kindly dabbing away her tears.

Using this slight diversion as a chance, Carol joined the conversation. "Welcome back to the household, Young Master."

Dylan smiled at her in response and nodded.

Three years was certainly not an insignificant quantity of time, and considering how old memories eventually fade with age, Dylan assumed that if he chose to live away from his loved ones long enough, his emotional connection to them would fade as well. However, that didn't seem to be the case. The memories he possessed of them, as precious as they were, didn't become any less precious simply because they were left in the hands of time. In truth, absence had made the heart grow fonder. He loved and appreciated those memories even more than he once had before.

He watched as Carol lifted a little bit of mashed potato from her plate into her mouth. Although she was eating, she wasn't consuming a substantial amount of food at all. Spotting his gaze, she gave Dylan a small smile, curious as to what he was thinking, but soon her smile grew faint.

Just like the pale skin upon her face, Dylan's heart became white as well. The three years he spent trying to forget about the woman who became his brother's wife crumbled apart in his mind.

✳ ✳ ✳

"I'm sorry, Young Master. I didn't think you would be in your room reading books," Samantha said as she lowered her head, embarrassed. She wasn't often the type to make mistakes, so she felt particularly flustered. Aware of this fact, Anna, who stood behind Samantha, lowered her head as well.

"I think it's more like you didn't think to knock on the door since this room has been empty every day for the last few years."

Dylan's tone of voice sounded like water flowing down a river. Anna raised her head slightly. He was sitting on a windowsill with the sunlight pouring in, his gaze still fixed on his book.

"I'm sorry," Samantha said.

"I didn't say that to hear you apologize. I'm just

saying let's both pretend we don't exist around each other and mind our own business."

Dylan's voice was the same as it was all those years ago. Anna felt relieved to hear it once again that a small smile crept up onto her lips.

At that moment, Samantha glanced at Anna. Nodding her head in understanding, Anna walked towards a closet built out of red mahogany wood with the intent to put away the clothes she was holding. She pulled on the closet door's handle, but for some reason it didn't budge.

Dylan quietly watched Anna struggle with the closet door and the heap of clothes she held, until eventually he closed his book and walked toward her. He clasped his hand over Anna's own on the handle of the closet and pulled together with Anna. Suddenly, the doors, which hadn't budged an inch under Anna's grip, flew open like magic.

Anna forgot for a moment that she was holding a bundle of folded clothes in her left arm and turned to look behind her. Since Dylan was standing right there, his arm bumped into Anna's, making all the clothes fall to the floor.

"I-I'm sorry," Anna stuttered. She immediately bent down over the ground to pick the clothes up off the floor. However, Dylan moved to bend over along with her, helping her out.

Samantha observed Anna and clicked her tongue in annoyance. Anna was someone that couldn't go a single day without causing a problem. If a different employee had made that same kind of mistake, they would've been punished by Samantha right away, but it was a different story with Anna. Samantha pretended she didn't see Anna's mistake, and continued watering the potted plants. Her actions seemed to indicate that no matter what kind of problem Anna caused, Samantha had no intention of scolding her.

Dylan's expression looked indifferent. "Fold these again and before putting them in," he told Anna, then he left the room.

Anna stared at the door Dylan left through for a moment before she felt the pressure of Samantha focus on her once more, so she immediately moved to refold the clothes as she was told.

Did he forget? she wondered. Dylan definitely saw her clearly, looking upon her with his own two eyes, yet it seemed like he didn't recognize her at all. *I hadn't forgotten about him for even a moment the entire time he was gone. Did he forget all about me?*

Anna timidly grasped Dylan's clothes as a disappointed expression overtook her face, holding them tight as if grabbing him by the collar.

✳ ✳ ✳

Only in the afternoon when the sun was crossing its zenith did Dylan have his first meal of the day. It was rather late. Since he couldn't decline his friends' invitation to a welcome party last night, he ended up drinking way too much. His hangover was stabbing him in the head with every step he took up the stairs.

At the height of the spiral staircase came a woman's rough voice, somewhat aged in manner. "Would you like me to bring you some snacks?" it asked.

"It's fine," came someone's response, clear but tired. Upon hearing it, Dylan recognized it as the voice of his sister-in-law. "It just seems like I don't have much of an appetite today."

"It's because you have a habit of eating like that every day. How about trying to make your meal portions a little bigger starting today? Even if you don't have the appetite for it, you must eat to live your life to its fullest."

"I'll try, then."

"How about some dried figs?"

The aged woman's quick thinking seemed to make Carol feel amused, since a faint sound of laughter came from above the spiral staircase. Dylan was glad that she was able to laugh like that, at least. He felt himself smile along with her.

"All right," she acquiesced.

"Please go to your room first. I'll bring it up to you right away."

With the conclusion of that statement, rapid footsteps began resounding down the stairs. They startled Dylan's smile into disappearing, and a flustered look adorned his face. He looked around himself to see if there were any good hiding places, but the woman descending was a little bit faster than him. She saw Dylan and flinched in surprise.

The woman herself, however, didn't seem to cast any suspicion upon Dylan as she simply nodded her head in greeting and continued on by. Thinking it over again, he didn't really have any reason to hide. He wasn't a suspicious figure. Dylan smirked in self-ridicule and began to walk up the stairs once more.

On the second floor of the house was a room belonging to Sir Crane and his wife, and David, Carol, and Dylan's rooms were on the third floor. The floors of the mansion were connected by spiral staircases, with one at the center and another on each end of the hallway. Because of this, it was safe to say that although Dylan lived on the same floor as David and Carol, running into Carol while walking through the house would be an unlikely occurrence.

However, today was different. Dylan had his meal at the underground level and intentionally avoided the rightmost staircase leading to his room to make sure he could keep from encountering his mother, placing him in Carol's path.

Carol stepped into the third-floor hallway with drooping shoulders. She was ignorant of Dylan following behind her.

The fact that Dylan couldn't do anything but watch Carol from behind despite her feeble and lonely countenance inflicted Dylan with a fervent pain incomparable to the headache his hangover gave him. She looked like she would fall over at any moment. If he could've, he would've immediately embraced her tight in his arms, but she was his older brother's wife, his sister-in-law. His older brother, David, was a man Dylan respected and looked up to.

Dylan didn't have the right to hold her in his arms. Not in this lifetime.

Thud.

Carol was walking down the hallway when she stopped for a moment. Then, she turned her head to the side, facing the open window on the wall. Dylan's gaze followed hers out the window as well.

In the middle of the yard was David, walking around. Walking beside him was a woman wearing a white apron.

Dylan's eyebrows furrowed.

The two people walked across the yard as if they didn't care about being seen by anyone else, chatting with each other in warm and friendly tones. When Dylan turned back toward Carol, he found her heading to her room, stepping through the wooden door with an indifferent expression plastered upon her face.

✳ ✳ ✳

Anna headed downstairs into the underground level of the house in a hurry. Thankfully, the rest of the employees were still lined up and waiting for Samantha's orders, as if preparations for dinner had only just begun. Anna joined them at the end of the line and stood with her back straight. Everyone who had already been waiting in line prior to her arrival shot her an intense glare for arriving late, but she pretended not to notice.

The firstborn son of the house, David, was late because he didn't realize how much time had passed while he was having a chat. Although Anna deserved to be chastised for getting paid without doing her job properly, Samantha didn't say anything about Anna's mistake this time, either.

"You–place the cutlery on the table. And you– help out Chef Hans," Samantha demanded, proficiently laying out orders and clapping her hands as if to guide the workers like sheep to their destinations. "You can go pick up the tools dropped on the kitchen floor, and the rest of you should start serving the food as soon as it starts coming out."

"Oh dear!"

However, no matter how frequently Samantha clapped the employees in the back and encouraged them to do their work, it was a difficult thing to rely on sheep to work as hard as she wanted them to. Anna had tripped over the carpet onto the floor while holding a pitcher filled with water, and upon seeing the sight of her, fallen, Samantha shut her eyes tight in annoyance.

The Kilner family had been sitting at the table and waiting for their meals, but now they were watching Anna. Madam Jane had furrowed her brows. She opened her mouth to start criticizing the clumsy worker before her, but a quiet yelp rang out from one end of the dinner table before she could speak.

"Shit!"

David had mistakenly spilled their aperitif, some white wine, onto the floor. Noticing it, Madam Jane swallowed back what she was originally going to say and quickly switched her focus onto the new mess.

"What are you all doing?" she asked. "Clean up the mess right away."

Since David had spilled his wine, Anna managed to avoid getting punished for her blunder. With a new pitcher of water in hand, she began to fill the empty cups on the table one by one.

Dylan kept his gaze fixed on her as she did so, eventually realizing that she was the woman who had dropped his clothes back in his room. She had porcelain skin and black pupils on a small face accompanied by delicate features. She struck him as rather beautiful.

"That should be enough," Carol told Anna. She spoke quietly, and upon hearing her, Anna stopped pouring water into her glass, giving her a small nod of courtesy.

Righting the pitcher once more, Anna moved on to fill David's glass. He hadn't glanced at Anna even once as he continued his conversation with Sir Crane, which Anna didn't mind at all.

Dylan clenched his hand into a tight fist under the table. Sir Crane and David were both deceiving Carol, and he could tell. He could see it happening right before his very eyes. He saw how his older brother had intentionally knocked the wine glass onto the floor earlier, causing it to spill onto the floor with a sweep of the back of his hand.

How dare he...! Dylan seethed to himself. He bit down hard on nothing, the muscles of his jaw becoming pronounced in fury. He couldn't bear to stay here casually having dinner when his mind was filled with disappointment, the sting of David's betrayal, and hatred for Anna.

Although he knew it was rude to do so, Dylan slid his chair back in the middle of dinner and stood up. The sound of the chair sliding over the floor was audible.

"I'm sorry. I don't feel well after smelling the food, so I think the four of you should have dinner without me tonight," Dylan said, an abrupt apology.

Then, he left the dining room.

✳ ✳ ✳

"Go to the library and find a book that interests you," David had ordered, so Anna left for the library on the fourth floor.

Usually, only David ever made use of it, so when Anna knocked on its door, it was only a mere courtesy on her part. Without waiting for an answer, she opened the door right away.

Once Anna stepped inside the large library, she inhaled deeply, taking in the scent of all the neatly aligned bookshelves. The smell of old paper and ink made her happier, and she smiled while navigating through the maze-like rows of literature around the room.

What book should I choose today? Anna mused, humming to herself contentedly.

David's order meant she could pick whatever piqued her interest. It was an order that he issued as a favor to her once a week, and it all began sometime in the past, when she had been cleaning his room. She couldn't control her curiosity and had secretly started reading a book that had been left on the table. When he caught her, she thought he would yell at her for touching his belongings without his permission. However, he told her that he had already finished that book, so it would be fine for her to take it to read for herself. In return, she had to read through the whole thing and bring it back to him personally.

It took Anna a whole week to finish reading the book. She visited David's room once she did to return it as he had commanded.

He stopped her as she was leaving. "How did you read it?" he had asked her.

"Huh? I read it with my eyes," Anna answered honestly. The fact that she gave such a simple and senseless answer made him laugh aloud in surprise, but at the time, she was just nervous. She was having a conversation with the first son of the Kilner family, after all. She had no idea what made him laugh as he did.

Afterwards, she shared her interpretations and understanding of the book with him, and they developed a closer relationship. Sometimes she would ask for explanations on passages that were too profound or deep for her to understand, and every time she did so, he would take care to explain things to her amiably, never appearing annoyed by her inquiries.

Ever since then, Anne had stopped believing the rumors about the Kilner family members claiming they were misers or tightwads cheap with their money.

Anna stretched her hands toward a book with a cover that proclaimed its title to be 'Yayok'.

"Is that a novel?" she muttered.

Although she didn't know exactly what yayok meant, the high quality of the book's black hardcover and the gold stitched lettering intrigued Anna immensely. A new book never ceased to make her giddy with excitement, so she opened the book and turned around immediately to read it, moving as if she were being chased.

Whump.

As soon as she turned, however, her hand bumped into the arm of someone behind her, making her drop the book.

"I'm sorry," Anna quickly said, bowing her head low in apology. She bent down to pick up the book, but the person she bumped into grabbed it faster than she could.

"Ya—yok," Dylan read aloud slowly. It was as if savoring the word in his mind.

Anna clasped both her hands in front of her apron and kept her gaze directed downwards. The gap between the two of them and the bookshelf was too small, so her body felt way too close to his.

"Was this a book you planned on reading?" he asked.

"It is," Anna hurriedly replied. "I picked it, but..."

Her response was vague and her words escaped her in a mumble. She was frightened at the prospect that Dylan might find the fact that she was borrowing and reading books from the library unappealing, forbidding her from ever reading any more books in the future.

"The title really matches you, actually."

Anna raised her head slightly. "What do you mean by that?" she asked.

"*Hah!*" Dylan sneered. "So you chose this book even though you don't know what it meant?"

Anna, dispirited, lowered her gaze back to the ground. Dylan's gaze seemed to belittle her, and his demeanor made her incapable of doing much else besides demure. He looked down upon her for a moment, his eyes cold, before he gave the book back to her. The thick book thumped heavily against her chest, pushing against it.

A low moan escaped her. "*Ah,*" she blurted reflexively.

"If you want to figure out what it means, read the book and see if you understand."

Anna held aloft the book that he pushed to her chest. She couldn't comprehend why Dylan was so angry toward her. Was he taking out his frustrations on her from earlier, when she messed up and dropped his folded clothes right in front of him? Or, perhaps he just didn't like the fact that she was in the library in the first place?

"If you ever hurt that person's feelings, I will pay back their pain tenfold," Dylan began, his eyes like a frigid fire ready to tear Anna apart. "I'll make you experience more pain than their heart could ever feel by ripping yours out of your chest. Behave while you still have the chance."

He left like a whirlwind after he finished warning her, and it was only after he was completely gone did Anna feel like she could finally breathe again.

She thought Dylan would definitely recognize her after coming back and she had been waiting for him every moment for the last three years. No one had instructed her to do so, but she planned to do her absolute best to pay back all he had done for her—the kindness he had afforded her—as much as she could upon his return to the mansion. Yet now he had a problem with her. What was it? How did she end up as the focal point of his hatred and anger?

Anna had to lean against the bookshelf to calm her racing heart for a long time before she could leave the library.

※ ※ ※

"Everything's turned completely upside

down!" Anna mumbled as she beat the laundry with a washing bat.

This had all begun once David and Carol chose to leave for a month to visit their parents. Not only did Anna's trustworthy sponsor disappear, but Dylan's started to treat her as a thorn in his side at all times. Her happy days around the mansion had come to an end.

"How am I supposed to wash all these clothes?!"

Although her arms felt like they were going to fall off from exhaustion, Anna couldn't do anything but continue to beat the laundry with the washing bat. The sky looked ominous and dark, as if it would rain at any moment. She tried her best to push away the thought that it might rain before she could finish. Samantha had told her to completely finish all of the laundry before the rain could start pouring down.

Unfortunately, not long afterwards, the incensed clouds in the sky started to unleash its torrent of droplets upon the ground.

"N-No way! Is it raining?"

Anna stomped her feet in frustration before rushing to collect all the laundry. She could hear the memory of Samantha's firm voice in her mind instructing her not to let anything get wet.

Stop crying, Anna thought, looking to the sky with resentment. 'The one who really wants to cry is me!'

✳ ✳ ✳

"Go to Master Dylan's room and see if his window is properly closed."

"M-Me?"

"Yes, you. Who else?"

Anna's expression turned pleading and she pointed at her soaked clothes. "I'm sure I'll get in trouble if I walk around looking like this, though," she said.

Samantha was away at the moment attending to Madam Jane's call. A girl with yellow hair came over, and Anna was worried she was going to be scolded for getting the laundry wet with the rain, but she ended up getting pushed into the metaphorical lion's den instead.

"And what does that have to do with me?" the blonde shrugged, smirking.

In the end, Anna had to put all her strength into wringing the water out of her hair and skirt before heading up to Dylan's room on the third floor.

Desperately hoping he wasn't present, Anna knocked on his door, but God didn't seem to be on her side because she heard Dylan's voice telling her to come in shortly afterwards.

Anna bowed her head low as she entered. "Since it is raining, I will close the windows," she said courteously.

Although he had been treating Anna like some parasitic bug disturbing his garden upon every encounter, he was pretty quiet. He must not have realized Anna had been the one to enter his room because he was concentrating on reading his book. She was determined to close the window and leave before he recognized who she was.

Samantha had told Anna once before that she had to put the flower pot on the windowsill down onto the floor before closing the window. Anna always considered having to do that as annoying as needing to serve every dish in a full course meal.

Crash!

Up until the pot fell and shattered on the floor, that is.

Even without turning her head, Anne could tell Dylan had stood up from his chair. She could feel it.

Anna desperately began pleading for forgiveness, despair encroaching upon her heart. "I apologize, Young Master," she said.

Before she knew it, however, he had reached her, tilting his head as he studied her dripping wet attire. She felt just as embarrassed as she would've had she been completely naked.

"You're a complete mess," Dylan said, and Anna hated that she couldn't reply to his insult. "I definitely warned you, didn't I? That I was only going to give you one chance?"

Dylan thought about what happened on the day David and Carol left the mansion by carriage. David pulled a white envelope out from his inner pocket, handing it to Anna, who then promptly accepted the envelope with visible glee. She placed it in her pocket, and as she did so, David lifted his hand calmly, settling it upon her shoulder.

Dylan continued. "I've been hearing from others that you've been making messes at work this whole time."

Undoubtedly, she had been able to get away with her incompetence because David continued to take her side, just like how he covered up Anna's mistake of spilling water yesterday by overturning his glass of white wine. Although she had shamelessly utilized Dylan's brother to her advantage, Anna still stared up at Dylan with an innocent look in her eyes, acting as if she were ignorant of her transgressions. What a manipulative woman she was.

"I treasured that plant," Dylan said.

As if to convey that she was willing to take any kind of punishment he would give her, Anna bowed her head. Dylan picked up pieces of the broken pot, scooped the dirt and the plant into his hands, and handed them to her.

"Hold it," he commanded. "Since you broke the pot, you'll be the pot instead."

Anna held the plant and the mound of dirt close to her chest.

Unsatisfied, Dylan frowned, furrowing his brows. He grabbed Anna's hands. "Lift it higher. Above your head," he said, as he positioned her.

"H-How long do I need to hold it like this?" Anna asked. He could already hear the whine in her voice.

"Until you announce that you will no longer

work in this household."

There was a frightening brand of sincerity in Dylan's voice as he spoke, leaving Anna confused.

✳ ✳ ✳

Carol was Dylan's first love.

The moment she entered the Kilner house holding David's hand, Dylan began to understand the true meaning of the words 'love at first sight'. He almost didn't recognize David standing by her side courting her and seeking her affection, so distracted as he was by her presence.

Even though he knew that it was impossible to ask for Carol's hand, she continued to occupy a larger place in his heart with each passing moment. Eventually, Dylan grew desperate for her love.

She would always act modestly, exuding calmness amidst a warm and friendly countenance. She looked transparent enough that one might fear she could disappear at any moment; it was almost as if, when reached for by hand, that hand would simply phase through her. Dylan believed his immoral thoughts would only taint such a lovely woman, so he could only watch her from afar.

The day after David and Carol's wedding, Dylan had no confidence in his ability to withstand living with them in the same house. The knowledge that they were now a lawfully married couple hung hauntingly over him. He ran away and didn't look back.

Three years have passed since then.

After reading the entirety of a book he found in the library, Dylan returned to his room. *At this point, she should have left the mansion in tears already,* he mused. Enough time had passed that the rain, which he had predicted would continue for the rest of the day, had come to a stop.

"You..." Dylan trailed off, astonished.

He was mistaken about the weather, but that wasn't the only thing he had mistaken. When he returned to his room, he found Anna still standing right where he left her, holding the remains of the broken pot's contents above her head. She looked like she had been there the entire time he had been away.

His forehead creased in displeasure. The plant was in a slightly lower spot from where he had positioned it for her, but it was still right above her head. As if to prove that she didn't cheat in any way, her forehead was dripping with sweat. She had bit down hard enough on her lower lip that it looked white as a sheet, the veins upon them made imperceptible simply by the force of it. Her entire body shook terribly, an obvious sign that she was reaching her limit.

Dylan couldn't tell if she was being tenacious or stubborn. "Put it down and leave for now," he eventually said.

No matter the motivation, however, her choice to endure simply looked foolish in Dylan's eyes, as if she had accomplished no better than outright disrespecting him.

Anna lowered her shivering arms following his command. She grit her teeth and tried to walk forward slowly, but she ended up merely wobbling and slowly collapsing onto a sitting position upon the floor.

Carol must have spent an even longer time in pain than you have suffered here, Dylan thought, refusing to spare Anna even the slightest glance. Anna strove fervently to stand back up, only managing after a considerable amount of struggling. She eventually left the room.

Quite a while later, Samantha entered Dylan's room to bring him tea. "Clean up that broken pot for me," he told her, but she only gasped in surprise.

"I will, of course, but... have you injured yourself in any way?" she asked. "Why is there blood?"

Samantha pointed toward the spot Anna once stood. There, on the floor, was a prominent stain of Anna's dried blood.

✳ ✳ ✳

Dylan sliced a piece of meat and glanced at Anna. She was standing at the ready with a pitcher just in case anyone needed her to pour them a new glass.

She hadn't been wearing any shoes, he had come to realize. He recalled the bloodstain she left behind on his floor and furrowed his brow. Her feet must certainly be in immense pain, yet her face remained impassive. Perhaps the wound wasn't as deep as he thought. Dylan shook his head. He needed to stop sympathizing with Anna. Although he felt a little bad for the fact that she had cut her foot on the shards of broken pottery, his determination to chase her out of the mansion before David and Carol came back couldn't waver.

Sir Crane and Madam Jane were the first to leave the dining room after finishing their meals. Dylan moved to follow them, but stopped to point at Anna and address her. "You," he said, "bring some herbal tea up to my room."

"Yes, Young Master," Anna answered with a smile. Although she was smiling on the outside, however, she felt extremely nervous on the inside, anxious at the thought that Dylan might be cooking up another scheme to punish her.

She put a pot, tea cup, and some herbal tea leaves she had grinded herself onto a tray.

Casey, a girl around the same age as Anna, walked up to her, smirking in derision. "All you need to do is make sure you don't mess up. What are you trembling so fearfully for?" she taunted. She was one of the people in the mansion who disliked Anna for having a sponsor backing her up. "You know, you've been worry free all this time thanks to Master David. Now it feels like you're finally being treated on the same level as we are."

"So it was you?" Anna asked. She smiled, her eyes curving up as she lifted her tray.

Casey's eyes twitched in annoyance. 'Why is she smirking at me like that?'

"You were the terrible person who'd skuttle up to Master Dylan and snitch on me every time I made a mistake."

As if she felt she had nothing to hide, Casey nodded her head brazenly. "Yep, that was me," she said. "So what? It's not like I'm the one who had to fix the mistakes I was telling him about."

"Would you be happy if I get kicked out of the mansion, too?"

"Yes. You have no idea just how much of a thorn in my side you are, and most of the other people working here think the same. Hey, let me ask you something since you're probably going to get kicked out soon anyway. What did you do to Master David? Did you sell him your body? Sleep with him?"

Anna's hands—still holding the tray—shivered faintly.

"I haven't committed any of the dirty acts you all imagine I have, but direct all your curses and your hatred toward me and no one else," Anna said, glaring at Casey with her teeth bared. "I can't stand having Master David insulted like that."

"Wh-who said I was? I was just asking," Casey replied, before she quickly left the dining room.

❋ ❋ ❋

Dylan sat on a chair and calmly watched Anna

steep herbal tea leaves in a pot of hot water. Considering how she still had yet to confess about the fact that she was injured, he assumed that not only was she stubborn, but she had a strong sense of pride as well. If that was the case, he just needed to push her far enough that her pride could no longer save her.

Meanwhile, Anna had no idea such thoughts were running through Dylan's head. Her mind was still a mess from her confrontation with Casey. What Casey had said to her was so ridiculous, so utterly absurd, that Anna had temporarily forgotten she was currently in the presence of an enemy.

Since it's not the truth, I'll just stop thinking about it, Anna resolved to herself.

Anna poured the tea from the pot into a small teacup engraved with a geometric pattern. Dylan held the teacup with his left hand. Anna had been standing on his left side, so when she stepped back, she bumped into his elbow just as he had planned. The tea, which had been lifted to reach Dylan's mouth, spilled over his lower lip and continued all the way down to his pants.

He immediately stood up from his seat. "Fuck!" he exclaimed. Because Anna backed away faster than he predicted she would, he had timed his movement incorrectly.

"W-what should I do? I'm sorry," Anna said. "Are you alright? Should I bring some cold water?"

She saw that the tea was still steaming and had immediately begun fussing over it. Dylan wiped away most of the tea on his lips with his sleeve, seething in fury.

"Do you even have a brain in that head of yours?" he asked.

"I really apologize. I didn't think to check where your arm was, Young Master."

"Every day you say you're sorry. I'm sick and tired of it."

Anna lowered her head, heart heavy with blame. "I'm sorry," she repeated once more. It was all she could say, after all.

Dylan looked down at the top of Anna's bowed head. He knew what he could do to completely destroy her pride.

"If you're really that sorry... lick it up."

"Huh?"

Just as he had expected, Anna's head snapped up, staring up at Dylan with a look that said, 'I must have misheard him.'

He wanted to confirm to her that she hadn't heard him wrong. "I told you to start licking," he ordered once more, his tone of voice vividly clear. "Leave it spotless."

Anna's wide eyes were shaking, almost as if she stood in the midst of an earthquake.

"What's wrong? You can't?" he continued. "Just quit your job, then."

At this, she clenched her hands into a fist. Quitting was easier said than done, and doing so meant putting Anna and her entire family on the line. Dylan might've been able to implement such a condition because he had been born into a rich family, but that wasn't the case for Anna.

Dylan smiled. Of course. He was certain she wouldn't go as far as to obey his absurd command. "If you have nothing else to say, then leave right now," he said, his smirk conveying his belief in the certainty of his victory.

However...

"I'll do it," Anna finally said.

What?

Before Dylan could even say anything else, Anna dashed over to him fast enough that she could've tackled him. Her hand came to rest over his chest, and before he could stop her, he felt her tongue touch upon the sharp angle of his chin.

After her hot, soft tongue tasted the texture of his skin, she shifted. Dylan could hear the tender sound of a tell-tale kiss as her lips pressed against the nape of his neck, sucking lightly and absolving him of the tea spilled upon him. Her eyes were closed, and she diligently attended to her task, licking his flesh clean with prominent sincerity.

Because of the unpredictable nature of her attack, Dylan was helpless to retaliate. The lewd sound and sensation of her warm mouth ran wantonly through his mind. He felt frozen, mired in place like a statue.

"I'm all done," Anna announced, pulling away. "I've licked you completely clean."

While Dylan was completely astounded, Anna had spoken with a calm, even demeanor. He came to his senses belatedly, backing far away from her and slapping a hand over his neck with one hand as he pointed at her with the other.

"Wh-wh-what did you—"

Anna's expression seemed to question why he was reacting like that. She had simply carried out his orders. And she did it with as much sincerity as she could muster, too. He was the one who issued the command, so why was he so surprised?

Dylan's face blushed a brilliant shade of crimson. "Get out. Get out right now! Out of my sight!" he yelled.

Surprised by his sudden shouting, Anna ran out of the room, escaping his presence without ever understanding what she had done wrong. From the tips of his ears to the root of his neck, Dylan was completely flushed. It was almost like he had gotten splashed by a tide of red ink.

"Damn it," he huffed. "I was ordering her to lick the tea on the floor, not..."

He looked down. His face wasn't the only thing that had heated up, it seemed. Glaring at his crotch, annoyance salient upon his face, Dylan insisted to himself that the big tent his pants now sported had been erected purely through instinct alone.

Primal.

A natural reaction.

It was certainly nothing born of his own volition.

✻ ✻ ✻

"Ugh, how do I chase this feeling away?!" Dylan angrily mumbled to himself.

He scrubbed at his neck using water from his bath, but no matter how vigorously he did it, the tactile memory of Anna's actions refused to fade. The feel of her tongue against him and the sensation of her hot breath ghosting over his skin kept popping up in his mind again and again, distracting him and driving him mad. After the incident occurred, Dylan would frequently find himself scratching away at his neck as his blood began to journey south, pitching another tent in his pants.

The same was happening to his body even now, sitting alone in the bath.

"She's deranged. Absolutely insane."

Poking above the calm surface of the bathwater, Dylan's rigid length continued to respond to Anna's memory. He stared at his member before grabbing it and shoving it back down into the water.

Since he had become like this for the last few days, he had stopped making progress on his plan to kick Anna out of the household. His older brother and his sister-in-law were set to return in three weeks, and once they did, he knew it would become much harder to get rid of her. He knew he had to hurry, but every time he saw her, he would recall the incident and the sensation of her sly tongue, poking out from between her luscious lips, would accost him once more.

Bothering him more than anything else, however, was the fact that he seemed to be the only one incapable of moving on from what had happened. It dealt a heavy blow to his self-esteem. He had meant to crush Anna's pride, but it was his own pride that had been crushed instead.

Dylan angrily slammed his fists into the innocent bathwater.

Later, after finishing his bath, he went back to his room and immediately climbed into bed. Also in his room was Anna, sweeping the floor with a broom.

His face contorting at the sight of her, Dylan pulled his blanket over his legs and picked up the open book he had left next to his pillow. *If it weren't for David and Carol, I never would've paid even a single ounce of attention to someone like you in the first place,* he thought as he began to read.

However, he kept glancing up at her periodically. She was focused on sweeping the floor and her lips were shut tight. It seemed like that was a habit she had whenever she was concentrating on her work.

Straightening her back, Anna swept her loose hair behind her ears. As she did so, her eyes met Dylan's, who had been staring directly at her. He was caught off-guard, and, completely surprised, he reflexively covered his mouth with a hand. His expression looked pained.

"What's wrong?" Anna asked, surprised as well. She rushed to Dylan's side, throwing her broom to the floor. "Are you hurt anywhere?" Uncertain of what to do, she studied his face and complexion.

Dylan glared at her as hard as he could. "This is all your fault," he said. If she hadn't turned around to look at him like that, he wouldn't have bit his tongue.

"What did I..."

Anna trailed off, eyes drooping low in sorrow. She was being blamed for something she hadn't even known she had done once more, clueless as to what her transgression could've been. At some point, she felt, he might even start blaming her for breathing. How was she supposed to hold up against it all?

After having focused on her work for so long, Anna's lips felt dry. She licked them, her tongue darting out to sweep across and moisten them.

Dylan began to shout once more, tempestuous. "Stop! I told you to stop!" His face was bright red and fury lay in his eyes.

"What have I done wrong? I won't ever do it again. Please, just tell me."

"No," he said decisively, voice ice cold. "There's nothing for you to know."

'Then what am I supposed to do?' bemoaned Anna. She couldn't possibly read his mind. She felt frustrated and annoyed.

"I bit my tongue because of you," he finally supplied.

Anna really couldn't understand it. Why did he hate her so much?

"Are you going to tell me to be your tongue this time, Young Master? Or are you going to order me to lick it instead?"

To her, Dylan had once been like a shining beacon of light descending from the sky. He had been the one to allow her to work in the mansion in the first place, and now, ironically, he was trying to chase her out.

He grabbed her arms. "Yes," he said, and before Anna could blink, he pulled her into bed with him and set her so that she sat upon his legs, looking down at him. He wanted to test how far she was willing to go. "If you can do it, then go ahead and try."

His hair was still wet from the bath and droplets of water clung to the strands. His piercing eyes, as cold and chilling as they always seemed to be when he looked at her, were now haltingly serious, glowering at her with palpable heat. His sharp, even nose was pointed high. He kept his lips parted, as if waiting for Anna to make a move.

Looking into his eyes, she finally realized he was being serious. However, if he was planning on striking fear into her heart with this command, he was sorely mistaken. What Anna was actually concerned about was something else.

Her heart suddenly started beating rapidly. A deep feeling began to well up in the bottom of her chest. This was what she truly feared most.

Although she had simply been matching

Dylan's gaze with her own, her breath started coming in quick, shallow puffs. The word yayok began to run through her mind; it was the same word Dylan had claimed suited her back then in the library, and she had since discovered it meant 'selfish desire'.

It matched what she felt now to a terrifying degree.

After breathing in heavily a few times, Anna slowly lowered her body, coming closer to him. Although she couldn't come together on his feelings and desires, this was something she decided he brought upon himself. As she closed her eyes and pressed her lips against his, pushing her tongue into his mouth, she kept in mind that she was just obeying his orders.

It's not my fault, she thought to herself. She was just being a diligent employee.

Dylan felt his tongue touch Anna's as he waited quietly, and for a moment, their tongues became intertwined. They shared each other's breaths.

Anna swore to herself, over and over, that this wasn't a kiss. However, Dylan grasped the back of her head and began to envelop her lips with his, leaving her mind completely blank.

It was definitely a kiss.

His lips pressed roughly against hers, and she wrapped her arms around his neck. His tongue felt molten, heatedly invading her mouth and exploring within. He grabbed her chest and Anna moaned, the sound vibrating between their locked lips. His other hand started slipping under her skirt, traveling up her sleek thighs toward her hips. It sought a secret place, edging deeper into forbidden territory.

Not there! Anna thought, alarmed, but just as she was about to push him away, a knock suddenly came from the door.

"*Ah!*"

The two opened their eyes at the same time, as if startled from a dream. Anna pushed Dylan away by the chest and quickly hopped off the bed to fix her clothes. Meanwhile, Dylan looked down at his hands as if he couldn't believe what had just happened.

What have I done? he gasped.

Anna adopted a calm, stoic expression, and it churned his insides into another storm. "I'll be taking my leave," she said, but he just glared at her, scolding her wordlessly. He waved his hand in the air, dismissing her.

Anna bowed politely and left the room. After her, another girl entered. "Master," the girl began, "I'll water the pot for a mome—"

"Don't. Just come back later."

After ordering her away, Dylan rubbed a hand across his face in self-recrimination.

✳ ✳ ✳

As soon as Anna stepped out of the room, she leaned against the wall and slowly slid down onto the floor. "Am I dreaming?" she mumbled to herself.

"I'm sure you'd want to think that," Casey answered sarcastically. She entered the room only to leave immediately afterwards, so she had heard Anna's stunned musings. Seeing Anna so breathless and out of her mind hadn't fazed Casey in the slightest. She believed that Anna completely deserved it. After all, Anna was probably going to get kicked out of the Kilner household eventually, and when that time comes, she would finally reap what she sowed and pay the price for her impudence.

"You're so disgusting," Casey taunted, urging Anna to give up. "If I were you, I would've left ages ago."

Anna stood up and faced Casey directly. "Must be nice," she said.

"What?"

"It must be nice to have the choice to leave, since, according to what you've just said, you can quit any time you'd like."

What does she mean by that? Casey thought as she scowled at Anna, her hands planted firmly upon her hips.

"I don't have a choice," Anna continued. "Even though it's dirty and terrible here, I have to endure it all and keep doing my best." She intentionally bumped her shoulder into Casey's shoulder as she walked by. "So, stop harassing me. Even if you pray to God every night, I'll never quit this job."

LEAH

Two

"There's going to be a party at Sir Tilda's residence, and they said they don't have enough hands to set it up properly. So, Samantha, pick some from the workers we have and send them over."

"Yes, Madam."

Madam Jane bit off some chicken meat and munched on it. She didn't have it in her mouth for very long before she frowned and spat the meat into a napkin in front of her.

"This chicken is undercooked!" she cried. Annoyed, she slapped her silverware down. "Dylan, dear, put your fork down. I'm not sure who it may be, but it seems like someone among our servants harbors an animosity toward us."

"My apologies. We'll replace the dish with a freshly cooked one right away," an attendant replied.

As the servings were ushered back into the kitchen, Madam Jane left her seat, claiming she had lost her appetite. Dylan, however, remained in the dining room, waiting alone for his new meal to arrive. He rested his chin in his hand with his elbow upon the table. Bored, he repeatedly poked the table with his fork.

"I don't have a choice," Anna's voice echoed in his mind. "Even though it's dirty and terrible here, I have to endure it all and keep doing my best."

Her words had been haunting him all night long, making him boil with anger. Did their kiss disgust her that terribly?

He frowned, his forehead creasing. If that were the case, what of the faint moan that escaped her after he wrapped his hand around her supple breast? Although he loathed to admit it, her lips were soft and smooth, akin to sweet, sugary candy whose taste only proved more addictive the longer he lingered. The more he kept kissing her, the more he forgot his original intentions, nearly submitting himself to the wild, carnal impulse that had begun to breathe motion into his hands and body.

He thought she had felt the same intoxicating cocktail of emotions he had, that he hadn't forced himself upon her.

Yet she says "dirty" and "terrible"!

Dylan unleashed the pent-up fury inside of him by stabbing the fork he held into the table. Hard.

Hearing the jarring sound of its impact, Dylan flinched and released his grip on it. The fork stood rooted in place, proudly upright and pointed directly at the ceiling. Samantha observed him fearfully and slowly stepped backwards.

"Y-Young Master is hungry," she said. "Get the meal ready quickly!"

✷ ✷ ✷

It was pleasant outdoors, so, with the warm sun shining down upon them, Anna and the other employees put up all the laundry they had to delay doing because of the recent bout of bad weather.

"Anna," someone called. "Master Dylan is looking for you."

"Me?"

"Yeah, he said that he got Samantha to get something for him, so he needs you to pick it up and bring it over."

"It's not a giant rock heavy enough to crush me with, is it?" Anna asked, genuinely worried. However, the person who came to fetch her just slapped her shoulder lightly and giggled as they walked past, assuming she was just joking.

She craned her head to look up at the window to Dylan's room. There, she spotted him leaning on the windowsill, watching her. Despite the fact that their gazes met, he didn't turn away.

Just a look at his face made Anna feel like she had caught on fire, her entire body burning hot beneath her clothes.

❋ ❋ ❋

Dylan watched the yard from the window for a long time. Amongst all the maids working on the laundry, he chose to focus on Anna alone, observing her closely. At first, he planned to withhold from her even the slightest amount of consideration before immediately kicking her out of the household. However, he knew he needed to be careful doing so, lest he risk damaging the good relationship he had with his brother.

In truth, Dylan respected his older brother more than he did his father. David was always kind, sincere, honest, and polite. Meanwhile, Sir Crane was someone that had devoted his entire life to making as much money as he could before he died. In contrast to Crane's indifference toward his family, David's support for them shone in stark relief.

It was because of this that Dylan was able to give up on Carol.

Unfortunately, Dylan's respect for his older breather had shifted into disappointment, and that was all because of Anna. A singular girl. Just what about her made David turn her way?

Dylan couldn't take his eyes off her. She was

CHRONICLES OF THE KILNER FAMILY

still doing her best to hang up the laundry in the yard. It seemed like that one rumor someone had circulated claiming she always tried to sneak off and rest whenever she could wasn't true.

However...

"She's limping?" Dylan murmured. He uncrossed his arms and narrowed his eyes, trying to parse her movements.

Anna looked troubled and her gait was uneven, but whenever Samantha called her name, she put a smile on her face and tried her best to execute the task given to her.

Dylan recalled the day he found some dried blood next to the remnants of a broken pot. 'Perhaps, it was on that day?' he wondered.

✳ ✳ ✳

Anna held a woven bamboo basket in her arms and knocked on the door to Dylan's room.

Knock knock.

"Come in," came his voice from inside. As soon as she entered, he pointed to a table as if he had been awaiting her arrival. "Put it there," he ordered.

Moving to comply, Anna kept her eyes locked onto the thin cloth covering the contents of the basket. Just as she had expected, it was hard for her to look at him directly. She had to avert her gaze from the bed as well, incapable of looking at it, either.

"If you don't need anything else, then..." she began, but Dylan stood up from his seat and pointed at the chair he was just occupying.

"Sit down. Here."

"Huh?"

"I'm telling you to sit down."

Anna finally glanced up at him to try and identify what kind of scheme he had to be cooking up, but he just cocked his head, nudging his chin toward the chair. She relented at the gesture and sat down with an uncomfortable expression on her face.

As soon as she did so, Dylan kneeled before her and lifted her skirt without any hesitation.

Startled, Anna brought out a hand to stop him. "Wh-why are you doing this?"

"If this becomes infected later on or something, you'll have to cut off your leg," Dylan explained seriously. "If you don't want to live your entire life with just one leg, you must take care of it now."

The absence of a teasing tone in his voice frightened Anna. It meant he wasn't trying to pull one over on her, and she quickly retracted her hand to give him access.

No wonder she gets hurt, Dylan thought. He noticed that the soles were completely worn out on the old shoes she was wearing. He pulled them off her with his own two hands.

"I'll do it myself," Anna protested, but Dylan refused.

"Stay still," he ordered firmly.

She squirmed in the chair as he continued. It was hard for her to get used to this sudden display of kindness after enduring his constant hatred.

The first thing he did was pull away the cloth scraps she had wrapped around her foot. The wound hadn't healed yet, so it was still bleeding. Seeing it, Dylan's expression grew dark and he hauled her foot up onto his knee without a warning.

Anna gasped in surprise. "P-please don't—" she pleaded. She tried to take her foot away, but Dylan moved faster than she could and grabbed her calf. The sensation of his powerful hand gripping her bare skin made Anna freeze into a block of ice.

His eyes narrowed, stern, as he spoke in warning. "If you keep acting like this, I'll make it hurt when I put the medicine on you."

Dylan took some ointment in hand and began to rub it over her wound. He was focused intently, taking care not to irritate the injured flesh.

Why did you act like that yesterday? Anna almost asked, but she couldn't bring herself to speak her mind, so she swallowed back the words.

"I'm done." Dylan slipped the ragged shoes back on her feet. Then, out of nowhere, he began to confess. "Half of this was my fault, but the other half was yours," he said.

Anna shook her head. "No. I broke the pot and stepped in it myself. The fault lies with me."

Her skirt had rolled up to her knee. Dylan took it and pulled it back down to its proper place, the back of his hand lightly stroking her smooth, pale skin. His eyes were dark, as opaque and fathomless as they were yesterday. "I'm not talking about the pot right now," he said.

Wherever he touched her seemed to tingle, goosebumps rising in place of a shiver. At last, it occurred to Anna what he meant, what the weight behind his gaze seemed to imply. He might've been tricking her, attempting to convince her to sleep with him so he could kick her out for it, or his intentions might've been genuine. Perhaps he did want them to spend a night together.

Whatever his motives might've been, one thing was for certain: he wanted her.

❋ ❋ ❋

"Please don't do this..." Anna mumbled, sleeping beneath a patchwork blanket. The blanket had far too many patches, its original pattern lost beneath every repair.

Dylan visited her every night she dreamed, and this night proved no different. Other people might consider having such a handsome young man occupy their dreams every night a wonderful thing, but Anna certainly didn't. Completely nude from head to toe, he approached her with only a small square handkerchief concealing the most intimate part of his body as if to taunt her, saying, "Curious, aren't you? You want to know what amazing things lie beneath this handkerchief, right? Makes you crazy, doesn't it?"

He fluttered the handkerchief around while teasing her, driving her absolutely insane. "I'm not curious," she vehemently denied. "I'm not curious at all."

"Liar!"

Just like magic, he manifested directly in front of her, his body beautifully toned. She couldn't keep her eyes from drifting down to gawk at his barely-concealed manhood. Nevertheless, Anna shook her head. "No. I'm not lying."

Dylan smirked devilishly, gesturing between his legs with a nudge of his chin. "Yet still, you specifically keep staring down here," he said, his expression annoyingly smug.

"No, I wasn't staring," Anna objected. She immediately shut her eyes. "I can't see anything anyways."

Despite her best efforts to shoo his visage away, his appearance still remained in sight, as clear as it was before she closed her eyes. She was still dreaming, after all. When she opened her eyes again, Dylan suddenly grinned at her brightly, making her deeply anxious. She swallowed back the saliva welling in her mouth.

His index finger and thumb, which were holding up the small handkerchief, slowly started to loosen their hold.

"No!" Anna cried in protest, just as the handkerchief gently floated to the ground. She moved to cover her eyes right away, but it was too late; she caught sight of the reveal. However, as soon as her gaze settled upon his crotch, unbelievable fury descended upon her.

He had underwear on the entire time.

Anna's eyes shot wide open. "You're wearing something!" she yelled, enraged.

Bewilderingly, Dylan was nowhere to be found. Instead, she was staring up at a familiar dilapidated ceiling, the likes of which seemed ready to collapse at any moment.

Suddenly, she heard someone hiccup beside her. Anna turned her head, finding her four-year-old younger sibling staring at her with the large, frightened eyes of a rabbit.

"No," Anna rushed to demure, "I wasn't yelling at you..."

Thud.

The potato her sibling held in hand fell onto the floor and began to roll away. The child's big, beautiful eyes quickly began to well up with tears. Panicking, Anna got up with the intent to calm and comfort the child, but her efforts proved fruitless. Her sibling cried aloud at the sight of her face, sobbing profusely. Anna knew that if she came any nearer the child would only cry louder.

In the end, all Anna could do was escape the house and leave the child be.

✳ ✳ ✳

Anna was beside Samantha, helping the older woman as she ironed some clothes. Whenever Samantha would request some water, Anna would reply with affirmation and spray the clothing. Then, Samantha would smooth out the creases with a heated iron.

There was going to be a large party in the village under the name of Sir Tilda. The two were working on the suit Young Master Dylan would be wearing to the party.

"Okay, this is all done," Samantha said to Anna. "Clean up and then bring this to Master Dylan before coming back. Make sure to take care not to crease it." She handed the gentleman's suit to Anna.

All of a sudden, Catherine, another maid, jumped between them and snatched the suit before Anna could grab it. Shrugging her shoulders, Anna just opted to concentrate on cleaning up.

In the afternoon, some workers were charged with heading over to Sir Tilda's residence to aid the household in their preparations for the party. "Let's go. Quickly, before we're late," Samantha commanded, and six servants in total joined her as she left for Sir Tilda's residence.

Sir Tilda's household possessed an overwhelming amount of capital, so they would often throw parties simply for amusement. Every time they did so, they wouldn't have enough employees to execute the preparations, so they would recruit workers from other households to make up for it. Although they had enough money to throw all these lavish parties, they were too stingy to employ enough workers so they could handle the workload themselves. The servants never got any extra pay for their efforts, but they opted not to complain too much because they were allowed the privilege of participating in the parties and taking home the leftover food.

"You two go to the kitchen. As for the rest of you, change your clothes and go to the main hall. Help out with the serving," said an older man addressing the visiting servants. He worked in Sir Tilda's household, and he looked to be in a position of equal prestige as that of Samantha in the Kilner household.

"May I go to the kitchen to help out as well?" Anna asked.

Of course, simply working at the party didn't guarantee getting any food. Not everyone could be so fortunate. If given the task of working in the kitchen, however, those chances would improve.

Unfortunately, the older man leveled Anna with an austere expression and simply pointed to the main hall, looking as if he would kick her in the bum if she dared to ask to work in the kitchen again.

"The guests will arrive soon," he continued, "so pour the champagne and place the glasses on the trays."

All the female workers wore a black dress with a feather on their necks and a white apron across their fronts. The dress was plain and cumbersome, long enough to cover the length of their entire bodies, and designed in such a way that the party's main guests would stand out more in comparison.

Crash!

Abruptly, the sound of glass shattering resounded through the air. When Anna lifted her head to the source, she found a girl who looked much younger than her, bowing deeply in apology. "I'm sorry," she kept saying.

"Get your head on straight!" someone yelled out. "They're coming!"

The shout seemed to Anna like the heralding cry of imminent war.

❋ ❋ ❋

Wearing a black suit, Dylan stood next to a friend of his, sipping on some champagne. The area was filled with laughter and cheerful conversation. Alcohol seemed to filter the world around the crowd, making even the worst jokes sound like the funniest thing anyone's ever heard.

"Hey, Dylan," said Chess, Dylan's childhood friend. "Where were you and what've you been doing this whole time?"

"You do know you're asking me the same exact question as you did when we met several days ago, right?" Dylan replied, uninterested. His eyes kept chasing after a certain someone.

"Is that so?"

"Yep, definitely."

"Who have you been staring at so intently?"

Dylan was leaning against a wall, watching something off in the distance. Chess followed Dylan's gaze and then broke out into a grin, smiling like an idiot as soon as soon as he realized who was occupying all of Dylan's attention.

"Beautiful, isn't she?" Chess asked.

"Yeah," Dylan replied absentmindedly. Then, he caught himself. "Wait, n-no!" he blurted, frowning.

As if I'd ever consider that girl beautiful, he thought, watching Anna stand around in her dull clothing, surrounded by guests in glamorous dresses and well-groomed suits. 'She's nothing to me but a headache.'

While Dylan's head was filled with troubled thoughts of Anna, Chess had assumed his gaze was drawn to someone else: Rin, one of the beautiful noblewomen amongst those Anna was serving. "According to Ena, most of the guys in the village have already confessed to Rin," Chess began. "They were all turned down, though. Her standards are so high that the instant she realizes she doesn't like the man, they're out."

Ena was Chess's sister. She was a couple years younger than him and best friends with Rin. He neglected to mention that, in the past, he had tried asking Rin for a date using Ena as a proxy, but he ended up getting rejected. Currently, Rin was wearing a red dress, looking like the fanciest woman in the party. Men's gazes followed her wherever she went.

"Should I try talking to her?" Chess asked.

Dylan shrugged indifferently, quite frankly uncaring. "If you want."

Chess started walking to Ena, joining her in the pleasant conversation she was having with Rin. A moment later, while Dylan was sipping on champagne with some of his other friends, Chess brought Ena and Rin over to speak to them.

"Say '*hi*'," Chess said. "I'm sure you all already know each other, but this is my sister Ena and this is Rin."

They exchanged a few short greetings.

"I'm Turner," one of Dylan's friends said. "I think we met last time. At that party held in Sir Sten's name." Turner politely bent to give Rin a kiss on the back of her hand.

"Is that so?" Rin replied coldly.

"I'm Dylan." Dylan smiled cordially and then followed Turner's suit, kissing the back of Rin's hand. As he did so, Rin's blood red lips curved up into a smile of her own.

"I've heard about you," she said. "You left home three years ago."

"I did."

"Are you back to stay?"

"For now," Dylan supplied vaguely. His response piqued Rin's curiosity.

"Does that mean you intend to leave again in the future?"

"If there are no unfortunate events forcing me to go, then I'm planning on staying in this village. However, life doesn't always go the way you want it to. I don't wish to be labeled a liar should the time come, so I'll leave my departure as a possibility for now," Dylan explained in good humor. However, as he spoke, he grew confused for a moment, caught off-guard by Anna's gaze meeting his own.

"I see," Rin smiled, nodding her head.

Rin and Ena then continued conversing for a good while with Dylan's group. However, since it seemed like all of Rin's attention was directed toward Dylan, Chess couldn't help but look a bit sad.

Noticing his friend's expression, Dylan tapped Chess's shoulder twice. "I'm going to rest for a bit before I go back home," he whispered.

"Why so suddenly?" Chess replied, incapable of keeping his pleasant surprise from leaking into his voice.

"Just 'cause. I'm a bit tired today."

"I understand," Chess nodded. "Be careful on your way home. I'll see you next time."

"Have fun in my stead."

Dylan asked the ladies of the group for forgiveness before leaving. Unaware of Rin's disappointment, he retreated, blending in with the rest of the party's guests.

✳ ✳ ✳

Anna tried her best to sustain the smile on her face as she served the guests of the party. Although her legs hurt, she knew she would only bring herself further down if she started complaining, so she hid her grievances.

She lifted a tray she held in hand above her shoulders and traversed the area. Bumping into guests and dropping the tray was always the servant's fault regardless of who might have stepped into the accident first, so servants always had to remain conscientious of their actions.

"Hey, bring a glass of champagne over here," someone called.

Anna came forward, heeding the request and presenting a group of young men with her tray. They appeared to be slightly intoxicated, having fun like the rest of the party's attendants, except they were chuckling amongst themselves as they looked upon Anna.

One of them was a man who was all skin-and-bones with a face like that of a snake. He stretched a hand out for Anna and his gaze locked on her like a serpent would their prey, sending a shock of unpleasantness down Anna's spine.

Crash!

While pretending to reach for some champagne, he brought his hand down upon the tray, making the five glasses perched upon it tip over and spill onto Anna's clothes as they toppled onto the floor one by one.

"*Ah!*" Anna exclaimed, surprised. She stared, stupefied, at all the glass shards now littering the floor.

"That's why you should be careful," the thin young man whispered. His voice sounded disgustingly slimy, creeping near Anna's ears.

"I apologize," she murmured. "I'll clean it up right away."

The older man from earlier, having heard the sound of the crash, came running forward, frowning with his forehead creased. He looked around for a mop and broom. Anna attempted to look for them as well, but he stopped her, informing her that changing her clothes would be of greater help to him. He indicated that she should head for the door and leave.

Anna bowed her head. "I apologize," she said once more. Then, she did her best to cover her wet dress by lowering her posture before escaping the party area.

The pungent scent of champagne coated her from the height of her chest to the bottom of her skirt. While shaking out all the droplets still clinging onto her hem, Anna mentally cursed the snake-like young man with all manner of bitter insult.

Nevertheless, she figured that perhaps this development might prove fortunate. Now, she could rest a little while she pretended she was changing her clothes before heading back into the fray. Anna was trying her best to think positively.

"Hey," came a voice.

Unfortunately for her, things didn't work out.

Anna could hear the sound of dress shoes clicking upon the floor as the young man who spilled the champagne approached her. "Since it was all my fault," he said, "I'll help you out."

He was getting closer. Anna could sense his ill intentions, so she backed away from him, fearfully surveying her surroundings. "No, the fault was my own. You don't need to help," she said, but the young man just smirked as if he found her amusing.

"What do you mean I don't need to help? You don't even know how I plan to help you."

"Regardless of whatever you're going to do, I'll be fine."

"Well, I won't. You ended up like this, so, of course, I should take responsibility! That's what gentlemen do, after all."

As if he was anything like a real gentleman! His eyes were akin to a predator's in the midst of stalking its prey, a malicious sparkle lingering within their ominous depths. Anna knew that if she were to make a mistake at this moment, something terrible would happen to her. She was terrified.

A moment of silence passed, then...

"Stop right there!" he shouted.

Anna lifted her skirt to keep from falling over it and immediately starting sprinting in the direction opposite of the young man. The further she fled from the party, however, the darker the hallways became.

Although the man was drunk, he was tenacious, and his determination to catch her had been sharpened into a fine, frightening point. It didn't take long before he caught up to her and seized her wrist. "I made you spill those drinks, so I'll help you change your clothes. Why are you running away?" he asked, chuckling lowly as he pulled Anna close.

She shrieked. "Please don't do this!" Intoxicated or not, the man was still, nevertheless, a man. He was stronger than Anna, and she didn't have the skill to fight him off. "Please," she begged once more, "Don't do this. Please!"

He dragged her by the wrist. Incapable of fighting him off, Anna could only scream as she struggled, fear made manifest in the frantic ring of her voice. The man opened the door to the room closest to him and forced her inside of it. "I haven't even done anything yet, and you're already telling me to stop. Quit whining!" he hissed.

He grabbed her shoulders and spun her around, forcing her to face him. His breath reeked of alcohol.

Suddenly, a different voice spoke out from the corner of the room. "What's all this?" it asked.

Anna instantly recognized it. Dylan. Dylan was here.

"Goodness," the frightening man huffed. "Looks like another gentleman's already claimed this room. Let's move this somewhere else, then —"

"Please, help me," Anna pleaded desperately.

Dylan didn't reply. The man lifted himself and renewed his grip upon Anna's wrist.

"Young Master, please!"

She was pulled out of the room with a jerk of her arm as the man shouted at her, demanding her to shut up. Turning to another room, he quickly entered it and threw her in. Anna cursed at Dylan and his feigned ignorance.

At that moment, someone ripped the man's hand away from Anna, kicking him brutally in the backside. The man toppled over with a loud tumbling sound and lay sprawled gracelessly upon the floor. "*Argh*, who are you?!" he groaned.

In a flash, Dylan sat upon the man's bust and began to nail his fists into the man's face. The thin man whimpered weakly, incapable of moving amidst all the pain. Dylan stopped, glared at the man for a moment with wrath burning viciously in his eyes, and then dismounted, leaving the man abandoned on the floor as he walked away.

Dylan took Anna with him. He brought her to the room he was initially resting in as she trembled in his grasp. "Pathetic," he cursed aloud. Fuming, he tore his tie from his neck with one quick, coarse movement.

Assuming he was addressing her, Anna felt insulted. "There was nothing I could do!" she cried. "He was the one dragging me around and throwing me in rooms—"

Dylan turned to her, baffled.

"—so why are you calling me pathetic? Picking out girls he doesn't even know and forcing them alone with him, drunk out of his mind—he's pathetic! Not me!" Anna screamed. Her back hit the wall and she crumpled to the ground. Tears streamed down from her large, round eyes.

"No, I wasn't—what I was saying was... I wasn't talking about you, but that scumbag..."

Dylan closed the distance between him and Anna, aware that she must have misunderstood him. She was wiping away her tears with a shaky hand; it didn't look like she would calm down, no matter what he said. He picked up the tall glass of champagne he had been drinking before he was interrupted earlier, handing it to her. "Drink it," he offered. "It'll calm you down a bit."

With him sitting by her side, Anna clenched her eyes tightly shut, taking the glass and gulping down its contents. She didn't stop until she emptied it.

The room was dark. Only silence remained, and neither of them tried to say anything. Dylan's right arm settled against Anna's left, and the slight touch distracted him too much to move away. He wondered if the scent of champagne he detected was coming from him or her.

It didn't matter, either way. He allowed himself to enjoy the light fragrance as he sat, idle, in the quiet of the room.

Whump.

At that moment, Anna's head fell onto his shoulder. The soft sound of her steady breathing only had to travel a scant few inches to meet his ear. 'No way,' Dylan thought, turning to look at her.

Drunk off a single glass of champagne, Anna had fallen asleep upon his shoulder.

✳ ✳ ✳

The next day, Anna spent the whole morning avoiding Dylan around the mansion, using her lunch break as an excuse to leave the Kilner mansion. After eagerly drinking the champagne he offered her last night, she opened her eyes to discover she was leaning on his shoulder after having fallen asleep. He had been sleeping there beside her.

She wasn't sure how much time had passed. The wall they were leaning on had a square window overhead with the moon peeking through from its perch up amongst the night sky. She quickly tried to extricate herself from Dylan, but then she got a good look at his soundly slumbering face. Unable to bring herself to disturb him, she stopped moving and stayed.

He had loosened his dress shirt by undoing its top two buttons and his head was resting turned slightly to the side. His position painted a picturesque image, akin to an elegant illustration inked carefully with a thin-nibbed pen upon an ivory parchment. His long lashes lay above his cheekbones, and although he seemed to be sleeping fairly deeply, it still felt as if his eyes could open at any moment and level Anna with a stern glare. Her gaze shifted, roving from his eyes to his high and well-defined nose, before drifting down its magnificent ridge, traveling across a path defined naturally by his unrelenting beauty. His rough yet soft lips, just barely grazing the moonlit shadow of his nose, looked mesmerizing.

Anna could feel herself start to hyperventilate simply from staring at him.

Her body remembered him, and she could feel the areas that had once been touched react to his proximity. Her nipples hardened into little peaks, and a dizzying heat began to pool down low between her legs. Muscles tensing, she had wanted desperately to just push him down and climb atop him.

Looks like I must still be a little drunk, Anna mused, shaking away the memory of last night as she bit her lower lip.

"Here they are," the elderly, bespectacled bookstore clerk told her, handing her two books.

"Thank you."

He gave her a white envelope containing her change. "Is this another errand for Master David?"

Anna laughed and nodded her head. David would often request her to buy newly released books he was interested in. He would put the money in a white envelope and tell her, "Again, I'll leave it to you."

He was a nice man, but be that as it may, she always made sure to keep some distance from him in the past while she waited for Master Dylan to return from his long absence. She wouldn't be able to forgive herself if he became the object of terrible rumors because of her influence.

✳ ✳ ✳

Arriving back at the mansion, Anna's first stop was at the library on the fourth floor. She needed to put back the book she had borrowed with David's permission as well as shelve the new books she had obtained from the bookstore.

Before heading inside, however, she knocked on the door. If it was Dylan's voice answering the knock, the plan was that she would just run away instead, but no reply came from within.

"Is there really no one there?" Anna murmured, doubtful. She carefully eased open the door and peeked inside, surveying the surroundings. Fortunately, she couldn't detect anyone's presence.

Letting out a sigh of relief, Anna entered. Foregoing the bookshelves near the entrance, she traveled to the deepest section of the library. She was humming happily to herself, looking for a spot where the book should be placed, when, suddenly, her keen senses alerted her to the sound of the library door clicking open.

Startled, she held the books she brought tightly to her chest as if doing so could somehow save her life.

Clack, clack.

The person who had entered walked leisurely, their steps resounding through the quiet room. Then, the steps halted, and Anna watched as a pair of hands pulled a book out from its perch in one smooth motion. She knew exactly who those big hands belonged to.

Why him out of all the people...! Anna thought frustratedly, banging her head lightly on a bookshelf. She blamed herself for entering in the first place. However, noticing that the sound of her head colliding with the bookshelf was louder than she thought, she flinched. *Did he hear that?*

She couldn't bring herself to move at all, her head stuck in a leaning position against the shelf, mid-head bang. Thankfully, Dylan didn't seem to show any particular sign of noticing her. After a couple moments, Anna slowly raised her head and began to carefully study his movements.

His long, thin fingers ran across the book titles without much intention, unperturbed. So, he really didn't hear anything. Overcome with relief, her legs started quivering. In order to rub some strength back into them, she bent over.

As soon as she did so, the books she held improperly in her arms slid to the floor, starting with the one that had been closest to her chest and on top of the stack. She didn't even get a chance to catch them before they tumbled loudly to the ground.

"Who's there?" Dylan asked.

Anna could hear him drop the book he had been holding onto a table. She hurriedly picked the books up off the floor, a troubled expression fixed anxiously upon her face.

Then, he found her hiding spot. "So it was you," he said, squinting, as a look Anna couldn't decipher crossed his features. "Why are you in here?"

"I had to deposit some books. After putting these away, I promise I'll leave immediately."

Dylan considered the three books Anna held tightly in her arms. He began to step nearer as he spoke. "I don't believe I've seen those before."

"These two have been recently purchased," she

tentatively explained.

He looked displeased by her response. "Who told you to buy them?" he questioned, although he already knew the answer. It was more like he was asking, "Why did David ask you to buy those books?" He told himself it didn't matter even if she told him the truth, but his mind was suffused with unease. "I assume it was my older brother."

Anna nodded. "Yes," she said. "Master David issued me this errand before he left."

Dylan's mouth stiffened, pressed into a terse, thin line.

Then, without warning, Dylan began to lengthen his strides toward Anna. Fearful of his sudden increase in pace, Anna retreated backwards until she stood flush against the wall behind her. He reached out, retrieving the book she was clutching closest to her chest.

"Have you read this one?" he asked, lifting it to reveal its title. Yayok.

Anna blushed furiously, embarrassment and humiliation greeting her in equal measure. Yayok started off with the heroine reminiscing about her dirt-poor past. In order to escape from her terrible life, she used her beauty, charisma, and wit to acquaint herself with governmental powers, engaging in illicit affairs with them to climb the ranks. She kept each of them on a tight leash so they would always remain fixated firmly upon her.

However, much like Icarus flying too close to the sun, her hubris got the better of her. Her life came to an end while she was having sex with a man she believed had genuinely loved her. One could claim that it was a stale old story about people paying for their bad karma, but that wasn't why Anna was so embarrassed.

It was because every prominent sexual encounter the heroine underwent was described with explicit detail. The fact that Anna chose such a sordid novel amongst all the other books in the library she could've read brought a cold sweat to her forehead.

"She's just like you," Dylan continued. The last time they met in the library, he had told her the same thing.

Anna shook her head in denial. "I'm not so sure about that. The main character of the book is... different from me. Very different."

"No, you're definitely similar." He swiped the last two books Anna carried and placed them upon the empty shelf next to them. Then, he closed the last of the distance between them, cornering Anna as she glued herself to the wall. "Why did you run away without saying anything to me yesterday?" he asked her, running an index finger down the line of her jaw.

Anna swallowed. "I didn't run away, I—" she began, but Dylan wrapped an arm around her hip and pulled her into an embrace. Her eyelashes trembled.

"Liar. For ages, you studied every inch of my face. Then you suddenly fled as fast as you could."

Her eyes widened in shock. He was awake at

the time!

"I—I was simply wondering whether I should wake you up or not..."

"That room was dead quiet, you know. Even without opening my eyes, I could tell. I could tell how hard you were staring at me; I could hear every heated breath that escaped your lips."

Anna's entire body was wrought with jitters. Dylan pushed his hips forward, prompting her to feel the firm press of his hardness against her.

"I'm sure you weren't aware of this, but I knew just what you wanted, the things going through your head upon every inhale. It made me end up..." he trailed off, allowing his lower half to speak for him. He pressed even harder against her and the rigid outline of his manhood atop her stomach felt impossibly clear to her; they may as well have foregone clothing entirely. Anna gasped loudly and shivered, causing friction to ride against his rod. The jolt of feeling caused him to furrow a brow. "You wanted me that night as well," he said.

Hidden in the farthest section of the library, Anna and Dylan stood in a dizzying embrace, their heated bodies held tight together, lingering between the bookshelves. She knew nothing beyond him. He consumed her senses. Even the smell of old books that usually perfumed the library, which she adored so much, evaporated from her mind, driven away by the force of the warmth between them.

"I—I..."

Anna struggled to speak. Before she could confirm or deny his claim, he dipped his head, enveloping her lips in a kiss. His lips felt smooth against hers, yet he kissed her with an insatiable urgency. Anna's hands, which had been flailing through the air, settled at last onto grabbing his shirt. She could sense the power in his form, the strength lying in wait within the muscles beneath his skin, and the thought shot anticipation through her gut.

The solemn library's quiet atmosphere was broken by their hurried gasps of air. They kissed so deeply it was difficult to determine whose lips belonged to whom. The wet sounds of their mouths meeting filled the room, their tongues clashing between them. This was by no means an illusion, but Anna felt as if she were in a dream.

Pulling back for a moment, Dylan began to pull Anna's zipper down her back. Now free from the kiss, she inhaled deeply, breathing in all the air she had lost to him as her chest rose and fell. He pulled her dress down so it rested below her stomach, exposing her perky, pale breasts. Licking his lips at the sight, he pulled her dress down even farther. His attentions made her nipples pebble, and they grew pert with aching desire.

It felt like every ounce of her was thrumming with barely contained energy.

Dylan lowered his head and began to taste her breasts, brushing his lips against her soft skin. Anna's hands had moved to a death grip upon her skirt, but the moment his warm mouth enclosed it-self over a nipple, she gasped, her hands flying up to bury her fingers in his hair. He licked the sensitive peak as if it were sweet candy, leaving his hot, moist tongue over it with enthralling finesse.

Anna looked to the ceiling as the sensations threatened to consume her. Dylan maneuvered his tongue deftly, sometimes teasing the tips of her nip-ples with a push of it. When he began to gently nib-ble upon them with his perfect, white teeth, how-ever, Anna couldn't hold back her moans.

"*Ah!*"

Hearing her passionate cries inflamed him fur-ther, and he doubled his efforts, lavishing her breasts with vigor and carnal determination. Before she knew it, his hands were underneath her skirt, groping her supple bottom.

Lifting his head up again, he observed Anna's flushed face, the way her breaths labored to escape her kiss-swollen lips. He captured those lips once more, thrusting his tongue inside her to coil against her own.

One of Dylan's hands began to slide off her butt to her thighs, edging toward the valley between them, and upon this realization, Anna braced herself by taking hold of his powerful arms. He pushed her underwear aside, his fingers stretching past her pu-bic hair in search of the sensitive secret they con-cealed.

He didn't take his eyes off her for a second. He took care to watch every little reaction she made.

The deepest part of her body felt hot and slippery, and Anna shivered uncontrollably, panting as she moaned. Dylan's middle finger found and began to softly stimulate the petite flower bud between her legs. Her arousal manifested in her face, blossoming like a beautiful red rose.

"Look at me," Dylan mumbled softly. His lips glistened with the slight sheen of their shared saliva. Anna obeyed, taking in his enchanting visage and sensual expression with her darkened, dilated eyes.

Suddenly, foregoing any warning whatsoever, he pushed his middle finger deep inside of her warm, dripping wet channel. She gasped, throwing her head back as she shrieked silently. Her expression contorted to reveal the pain she felt at the intrusion.

Still holding tightly onto his arms, Anna started shedding tears clear and beautiful enough to compel anyone who saw them into licking them off her face. As she stood sporadically gasping in pain, Dylan pushed one more finger inside.

"*Ah...!*" Anna balled her right hand into a fist and smacked it against his chest in resentment.

"Lift your head and look at me," he commanded once again. She was still floundering with the pain. It felt as if her body was being torn into two. "Now," he said, and his voice began to sound as if he were begging.

Anna slowly lifted her head and looked at his face. He seemed as pained as she was.

"I know it hurts," he continued, "but if you

don't do this now, it will hurt even more later on." His left hand moved to cup her chin and her head naturally tilted to look up at him. "Close your eyes. I'll do it slowly, so try your best to focus on the sensations."

Anna licked her lips and quickly nodded her head, shutting her eyes tightly. She couldn't help the whimpers that escaped her as soon as his fingers started moving again. It still hurt, but as more time passed and his fingers continued to swirl around inside of her, massaging her inner walls, Anna's reactions began to change. Sensing this, Dylan started moving his hand a little more roughly.

In comparison to the overwhelming discomfort she felt at the start, she was doing considerably better, now able to fit two of his fingers inside of her. They were coated in her slick juices, dripping hot and sticky from where they were submerged.

Anna was braced with her back flat against the wall, her chest heaving laboriously up and down. Soon enough, distracted by sheer sensation, she didn't realize that she had already begun to grind her hips against his hand.

Dylan's left hand briefly caressed one of Anna's breasts before reaching down to cup his throbbing hard-on, which strained prominently against the restrictive fabric of his suit pants. Watching her completely lose herself to the intense ecstasy he gave her made his body thrum with overwhelming excitement. He could barely hold back. 'Just a bit more. Just a bit more,' he thought to himself. He had to make sure she was perfectly ready to take all of him inside her before he went any further. However, his body was already reaching its limit.

Feeling pained, his body thoroughly seized by the ache of arousal, Dylan pulled out his fingers. Anna wobbled as if she would fall over at the loss, so he kissed her forehead as he unzipped his pants. His once-hidden manhood appeared to literally bounce out of its confines. Her eyes widened at the sight of it as she barely managed to keep herself upright upon her shaking legs.

His shaft was much larger than she had ever imagined. Thick veins entwined the length of it, looking as if they were ready to pop out. She was finally seeing, with her own eyes, the very thing that the Dylan of her dreams used to tease her with every night, saying, "Should I show you or not?"

Anna shivered again, this time in fear, as a renewed sense of danger descended upon her. Dylan lifted one of her legs to rest upon a table. He was preparing to get into position between her legs, one of his hands holding onto his turgid length.

"Wait!" she suddenly cried, pushing at his chest and removing her leg from the table.

Anger descended upon Dylan's features, but after having seen his intimidating package, Anna could only think of all the dreams she had woken up with this morning. At the same time, the face of her sobbing sibling, frightened by her dream-induced sleep talking, crossed through her mind. "I'm sorry. I can't do this," she said.

She started to pull her clothes back on, a guilty look on her face. Confusion and disappointment washed through Dylan. He smiled bitterly. He was still incredibly turned on and hadn't been given the chance to calm down or satisfy his arousal.

Anna pulled up her dress's back zipper and glanced up at Dylan, whose clothes were similarly disheveled. His eyes and his raging hard-on looked as if they would burn her alive with the combined force of their scorching passion.

"I'm sorry," she repeated, looking away.

"You're the only one who's enjoyed it so far, but now you're telling me no?"

She would've apologized again, but she didn't have the strength to. Even just telling him she was sorry made her feel guiltier.

"Get away from me," he said. "From now on, never show yourself around me."

He was furious at her. Anna couldn't say anything in response, nor could she retaliate. Wordlessly, she exited the library and left him behind.

Three

Madam Jane took a thick, white slice of fish steak and guided it to her mouth with a fork, chewing it. "Is the food not to your taste, Dylan?" she asked, looking to her youngest son. It seemed as if he hadn't heard her in the slightest, cutting his fish steak into smaller and smaller pieces. "Dylan," she said, this time with a sterner and determined tone.

He finally raised his head to meet his mother's eyes.

"It looks like you haven't been eating at all these days. Are you worried about something?"

Dylan shook his head. "Not at all," he said. "I simply don't have the appetite."

"I'll make sure that tonight's dinner will have that meat dish you really like, then."

He nodded. Then, he put his fork down onto the table. "I'll be taking my leave first."

He slid his chair back and left the dining room. Sir Crane and Madam Jane, left behind, exchanged glances with each other.

"He's acting like he used to back then, isn't he?"

"That's right. Just like he used to three years ago," Madam Jane sighed, propping her head up with her hand.

At the time, he announced that he wanted to leave the household and go on a trip out of the blue, looking like half his soul had left him. Although his parents asked him what was wrong, he simply kept his mouth shut tight, as if he had forgotten how to speak. He confined himself to his room to stew amongst his own thoughts and ate so little that he lost a considerable amount of weight.

Dylan was showing similar signs now, bearing something akin to the disconsolate expression he used to wear in the past.

"He's not going to tell us he's planning on leaving again, is he? If he does, then I'm going with him. I can't just let him stray so far away from us again!" Madam Jane cried loudly.

Sir Crane frowned and shook his head. "Dylan is an adult. That means he has the right to choose his own future. And, on top of that, it's not like we're the ones sending him away. It would be his own conscious decision to do so," he said, lifting a glass of water. Although his words sounded cold, his face echoed the worry etched on Madam Jane's face.

"That's why we let him go back then," she argued, "but it hasn't even been that long since he came back! He might've disappeared for only three years the first time, but there's no guarantee he'll take as long the second time. He might not come back until thirty years have passed!"

After Dylan left, Madam Jane hadn't gone a single night without worrying. She was unable to sleep restfully, burdened by the thought that he might not have been eating well or that he might've been going through hardships. Her worries beget more worries, and her imagination began to supply her with an endless array of worst-case scenarios.

Madam Jane started to sob. Sir Crane slid a handkerchief across the table to settle in front of her. "It's not like we don't have a means of keeping Dylan here," he told her.

"You're saying you have an idea?" she asked, doubtful.

"Of course."

"What is it, then?"

"We just hasten the process of getting Dylan married. Once he obtains a family of his own that he needs to take responsibility for, and fathers a child, he would never even dream of leaving on his lonesome ever again. He's not heartless, after all. And he's of marriageable age, as well."

Madam Jane completely agreed with Sir Crane's plan and nodded strongly in support of it. "You're right," she said. "We should look for an eligible girl to join our Kilner family right away." Motivated, she shot up from her seat, looking as if she could somehow get Dylan married the very next day.

"Let's finish our meal first."

"How can you sit there and eat when you're a parent? We can't waste a single precious second!"

"No, but wait—"

Madam Jane lifted her heavy frill dress by the sides and fled the dining room. Sir Crane watched her go and, smiling bitterly, set his fork down despite the hunger he felt. All the employees looked upon him with pity.

* * *

Anna was dutifully following Dylan's command of never showing herself in his presence. Whenever Samantha gave her a job related to him, she would make an excuse like her stomach suddenly felt bad or she had a headache. If Samantha still insisted upon giving the job to her, she'd pass it onto someone else, presenting it to them as if they were Samantha's direct orders. She never took any paths that might've led to him and avoided the stairs by his room.

However, the longer Anna continued to avoid Dylan the lazier she seemed. It began to look more and more like she was making up excuses to avoid work, so she ended up getting reprimanded by Samantha with increasing frequency.

"I know I definitely told you to come to the dining room, so why are you here mopping instead?" Samantha scolded.

Today was one of those days.

Samantha had spotted another worker in Anna's place in the dining room, so she had sought Anna out in anger, finding the latter in the midst of cleaning stairs on the second floor.

"Are my orders just a joke to you? Huh?" Samantha asked, raising her voice and pointing a finger at Anna. "You're completely ignoring me just because Master David's protecting you a little!"

"No, not at all. That's not the reason at all," Anna said. It looked like Samantha wasn't going to let her get off easily today.

"If that's not it, then tell me why. Why aren't you following my orders?"

"I'm sorry."

"Don't just say sorry! Explain to me your reasoning!"

Samantha smacked the mop away from Anna's grip and tossed it to the floor. Anna wasn't surprised by Samantha's hostility, but, nevertheless, she squirmed with indecision, uncertain as to what she should do.

"It's because I told her to," came a man's voice.

It started Samantha. 'Did Master David come back?' she wondered fearfully. However, the man who spoke ascended the spiral staircase, revealing himself to be not David, but Dylan.

"I told her to behave like this. Do you need any further explanation?" he continued.

Anna couldn't bring herself to lift her head. She could feel his gaze locked onto her.

"Ah, i-is that so? Then you should have told me, Anna... I didn't know that was the case and..." Samantha trailed off, shrinking away by the force of Dylan's glare. It felt as if the tables had turned and she had suddenly become the guilty party. If one really thought about it, however, this whole misunderstanding was Anna's fault in the first place for not speaking up and telling Samantha the truth.

The hatred Samantha already bore toward Anna began to grow. She became suspicious, convinced that Anna had intentionally withheld the truth to tease and trick her.

"Then, it's fine now that you know," Dylan said, walking past the two women and continuing his way up the stairs.

As soon as his footsteps were no longer audible, Samantha turned to Anna with fury still blazing vividly through her, looking even angrier than before. She took a few deep breaths before glaring at Anna one final time as if to convey precisely how much she wanted to rip the younger woman into pieces.

Without saying a word, she stomped loudly down the stairs a moment later.

✳ ✳ ✳

Dylan rubbed his chin, a serious expression upon his face. He looked so serious that anyone watching could've assumed he was in the midst of making one of the most important decisions in his life.

"These are our shop's best sellers," the owner of the shoe store said, holding up a pair of sharp-tipped manilla shoes. Dylan had been ruminating on what pair to buy for ten straight minutes now.

However, he shook his head firmly in rejection, disregarding the owner's suggestion. "I'm looking for a shoe without a heel that can be worn comfortably."

"Ah, is that so? Then, how about this? The heel is low, but its design nevertheless maintains a sense of style. This shoe is quite popular as well."

Unfortunately, this design didn't satisfy Dylan either. "The red coloring is way too flashy," he said.

The owner threw both his hands in the air, giving up on trying to satisfy Dylan's fickle tastes. Instead, he shifted his attention over to shooing away the flies that had drifted over from the fish mongering shop next door with a folding fan.

After a long while of arduous contemplation, Dylan finally found a shoe he liked. "This seems good," he said, indicating a simple black, low-heeled shoe devoid of any embellishments or adornments. It was the cheapest of the store's most frequently sold designs.

The store owner had assumed that Dylan would

buy something expensive due to his high-quality attire, therefore, seeing as Dylan ended up picking something cheap, the store owner couldn't prevent the disappointment from showing on his face. "If you're willing to buy it, then we need to know the size of the person who'll be wearing it," he eventually supplied. "Do you perhaps know their foot's length or width?"

It was probably the width of a hand's palm...

Dylan had finally managed to find a good shoe to buy after much deliberation, but now he was faced with another problem. As he struggled to answer, someone from behind him tapped his back.

"Looks like you're here to buy some shoes," Dylan heard them say. He turned, discovering that it had been Rin. She wore white gloves and held a flashy parasol in her grasp. About a foot behind her stood a young girl who seemed to serve Rin as a handmaid.

"Yes, well..." he trailed off.

Rin wanted to figure him out. "Is that the pair you chose?" she asked. "They look like women's shoes. Are they a present for your mother?"

"No. Among those that work in my family's mansion, there is a girl who had been injured because the soles of her shoes had worn out. These are for her."

"Oh my, is that so? How kind of you." Rin's suspicions ebbed away and she smiled happily. "Is there something wrong, though? You have the shoes, yet you don't look so good."

"Well, I do have them, but... I don't know her size, so..." Dylan trailed off once more. "If it's not too much trouble, could you help me out?"

Rin looked at him, a tremendous idea popping into mind. She walked to a chair inside of the shop. Taking off her high heels, she shyly lifted her bare feet from beneath her skirt.

Dylan knelt down on one knee before her. "Excuse me, then," he said, as he grasped her foot with his bare hands.

At his touch, Rin flinched slightly, a shiver running through her. His large hands explored every inch of her foot, exciting a ticklish feeling upon the skin found there. It seemed almost as if all sense of feeling had collapsed outside of where his hands lay upon her. Rin stared at them and the powerful veins that crossed their backs, swallowing back her saliva.

However, these strange sensations didn't last long for her. The store owner came over, ignorant of the situation playing out. "Now then, do you think you have a general idea of the size?" he asked.

Dylan carefully placed Rin's foot back into her heels. "It looks like a palm's width would be fine," he said. Rin's foot seemed longer and wider than Anna's.

Just as Dylan was about to pay for the shoes, Rin slid into place beside him. "Thank you," he told her. "I was able to order a proper pair thanks to you."

"It wasn't like I was helping you out for free, though."

"Hm?"

"I'm not a merciful enough person to stop in the middle of the street and give up my time for nothing in return."

Rin's unexpected deceit made Dylan confused and flustered. Seeing him in such a way drove her to laughter. "It's a joke! You don't need to get all out of sorts," she said.

"No, you were right. Since I've received your help, I definitely need to pay you back. I have nothing to give right now, so... would you like to pick a shoe?" Dylan gestured to all the shoes that were on display.

"I'm not one for declining people's gifts, so I'll go ahead and accept your offer," Rin smiled. She chose the neat little red pair that had been catching her eye for a while now. However, while they were nice, she knew she couldn't choose the shoe she truly wanted, for it was expensive, extravagant, and definitely not the right thing to pick in a situation like this.

Seeing that Rin had settled on the shoes he had been trying to recommend to Dylan earlier, the owner of the store gave her a thumbs up for her discerning eye. "You really have a knack for spotting great shoes," he said to her loudly, as if purposefully intending for Dylan to hear.

However, Dylan was only focused on inspecting the black shoes he'd bought for Anna. They were packed into a box after he finished paying for both pairs, including Rin's. He didn't seem to care much about the shoes Rin picked out, so a pang of sadness secretly struck her heart.

She fell into step beside him after they exited the store. "Do you think these will look good on me?" she asked him.

"There's nothing that wouldn't look good on you," Dylan said, and only then did Rin's smile return.

Since you bought me these shoes, I'll buy you a meal, she was about to propose, but Dylan spoke sooner than she could.

"Then, I'll be taking my leave now." He bowed slightly toward Rin. They reached a fork in the road, and on his face was a tender smile. Rin couldn't take her eyes off him, mesmerized. "See you next time."

After a moment, Rin finally came back to her senses. She managed, at least, to bend her knees and curtsy a bit in farewell.

✳ ✳ ✳

"Get some sausages before you go!"

Anna had gone out to buy ingredients for dinner. One of the store owners' cries had caught her attention, so she walked toward their butcher's stand.

She stared at the sausages hanging off the ceiling of the stand. While trying to gauge whether or not they were fresh, it occurred to Anna how similar they looked to Dylan's own 'sausage'. "Absolutely crazy," she mumbled to herself.

The woman tending to the butcher's stand

raised a brow. "What'd you say?" she asked.

Ah, I didn't mean it like that! Anna thought. She practically ran away then, fleeing to a vegetable stand instead.

Releasing a sigh of relief, she recalled her mother's earnest request to pick up some asparagus. As she began to do so, a middle-aged woman looking over the carrots beside her decided to comment on them.

"These carrots look particularly strong and sturdy today!" she said.

That was right. Master Dylan's shaft was just as sturdy as the carrot that the middle-aged woman held in her hand.

No, actually... Master Dylan's looked just a bit stronger...

"Crazy. Insane," Anna murmured.

The middle-aged woman heard Anna. She put the carrot back with the rest of the carrots on display. "Are you really calling me that?" she asked, folding her arms in annoyance.

"No, I was just talking to myself," Anna explained quickly. "I was distracted and..."

Once again, Anna couldn't do anything but hurriedly leave the store. She tried her best to focus solely on the question of what she should buy for dinner that night.

"Freshly baked baguettes, here!" someone yelled.

"Yep, just as I thought. Bread is the most convenient."

A crowd of people was forming, drawn by the scent of freshly baked bread. Anna joined them. The length of the baguettes seemed to stretch all the way from the tip of her finger to her elbow.

One of the people in the crowd spoke up. "They seem a bit short today for some reason?"

Anna's inner thoughts shot out of her mouth. "*Wha*—you call that short?" she blurted. Hot glares descended upon her from people all around.

Someone from the crowd pointed at the shorter baguettes and said, "Buy the short ones if you like them so much."

"N-no. Well, I do like the longer ones more—I mean, not that kind of 'longer ones', but long baguette breads. I mean—well—wait, what am I even saying right now?"

People stared at Anna as if she were crazy.

At the center of the world... no, inside of Anna it remained. Everything was connected to that in the end. Even upon having just a few of his fingers inside of her had driven her to ardent arousal, leaving her sopping wet. She had since begun to wonder what it would feel like if his entire length had actually entered her, and her frequent lewd thoughts of it made her certain she had gone mad.

She seriously wondered if she should go visit a doctor, but she knew she couldn't bring herself to explain her symptoms aloud. Swinging an empty basket back-and-forth in hand, Anna lowered her gaze to the ground in shame. A deep, repentant sigh escaped her. It felt like she had already sighed ten times today.

Not long after Anna had started walking again, a young child's desperate voice began to resound through the air. "*Argh!* Please, don't do this! It was my fault. It was all my fault!"

A group of people began to encircle an incident occurring down the road. "Is there something happening?" they asked. "It sounds like someone is being bashed."

"I was so hungry!" the child cried. "I'm sorry! I won't do it again, Father!"

People came running from behind Anna, pushing past her to get a closer look. She got mixed into the growing crowd.

In the middle of the road was a young boy who looked to be about ten years old, kneeling in front of a man whom he addressed as his father and begging desperately for forgiveness. The man wobbled as he spouted unintelligible curses at his child. Then, he took a swig from his bottle, which was wrapped in a paper bag.

"You little weasel! Learning bad things from your mother! You couldn't find anyone else to pickpocket, so you steal from your own dad?!" he slurred furiously, tossing his now-empty bottle to the ground. The crowd and the child both flinched and stepped back.

The man began to walk toward the child, an intimidating expression upon his face. The child screamed aloud, wrought with terror. Anna looked around, finding no one willing to help out the poor kid. He was on the ground, trying to scoot as far away as he could with his eyes clouded by tears.

The man lifted the boy up by the collar then threw him violently back onto the ground.

"*Ah!* F-Father!"

The child tried to yell out his father's name, but his father was already lost to him. The man was out of his mind, wholly intoxicated. Some of the onlookers merely clicked their tongues in disapproval, while others stood anxiously on the sidelines like Anna, just watching the terrible scene unfold before them. They were all the same. No one dared to interfere because they were scared of getting hurt.

"It's not over yet!" the man roared, closing the distance between him and his child once again.

Anna began to shake terribly, but that hesitancy lasted for only a moment. She saw the man lift his large hand up to the sky as if it were a blade forged to strike the young boy and she immediately sprang forward from her position, rushing toward the child and wrapping him securely in her embrace.

She clenched her eyes shut in anticipation of the attack.

Wham!

She heard it, but the sound of the impact differed from what she had assumed it would be. Perhaps it was due to how large his hand was? Regardless, she would soon lose consciousness due to the overwhelming pain. Then, once awakened, she would have a huge bruise on her cheek. She would need to hide that bruise in fear of embarrassment for

CHRONICLES OF THE KILNER FAMILY

days until it finally faded.

Yet... Anna felt no pain. None at all.

The crowd began to murmur. Whispers of a familiar name drifted from their lips.

"Looks like he lost consciousness."

"Wait a minute. Isn't that the Kilner family's youngest son? Young Master Dylan, right?"

"Hey, shouldn't we notify the Kilners about this?"

Slowly opening her eyes, Anna tried her best to comprehend the unbelievable situation before her. "Master?" she called out in a small voice.

Dylan had collapsed onto the ground. Blood was pouring from his nose and his left cheek was swollen, marked red by the shape of the drunken man's large palm. The man in question was looking back and forth between his hand and Dylan, over and over, the horrible mistake he had just made slowly dawning upon him. His angry complexion drained of color until his face was white as a sheet. Then, he promptly turned tail and ran from the scene.

Anna knelt beside Dylan, her hands hovering above his face and trembling uncontrollably. "Call for a doctor," she began, but her voice didn't come out right. She swallowed back the lump in her throat and tried again, louder. "Someone, please! Call a doctor!"

✳ ✳ ✳

When Dylan opened his eyes, everything around him was shrouded in complete darkness. Was it all a dream? He tried to move his body. As he did so, something on top of his face slid off and his sight returned to him. A familiar ceiling loomed over him.

Noticing that Dylan was opening his eyes, Sir Crane and Madam Jane, who had been looking after him, shot up from their seats.

"Dylan! Are you alright?" Jane asked. "Are you okay, my baby?"

The doctor with them spoke up in Dylan's place. "He had simply lost consciousness due to shock. He is now awake, so you need not worry anymore." As soon as the doctor finished their explanation, they left the room.

Dylan lifted himself up, his upper body rising. On one side of his pillow lay a wet towel. It had been placed on his face to help cool down his swollen, overheated cheek, and it had fallen off after he had woken up.

"What happened? Hm? Please tell me," Madam Jane pleaded. "You hadn't lost your voice or forgotten how to talk or anything, right?"

Dylan looked around the room. "No, I'm fine," he said. "What happened to the others that were there?"

"You think this is the time to be worrying about other people? The only person there who'd been bleeding out was you. I haven't received word of anyone else getting hurt."

That meant that Anna hadn't gotten hurt after he went down. Dylan breathed a sigh of relief and tried to remember everything. It seemed to happen so fast.

After impulsively deciding to buy Anna some shoes, Dylan had started walking back home, trying to come up with a natural-sounding excuse to use when giving the shoes to her. There had been a group of people forming in the middle of the street, however, and they were gawking at what seemed to be a fight, jarring him out of his musings. He had glanced over at the crowd without giving it much thought, but that changed when he spotted Anna amongst them.

His happiness at the sight of her was short-lived. Her legs were trembling and she had looked desperate to spring into action, which made him worried that she would try to intervene. Dylan parted the crowd and pushed himself inside of it.

Beyond the onlookers stood a large man wobbling on his feet as he threatened a young boy. The dangerous man had lifted his hand to strike the child, and at that moment, Dylan could hear the crowd's frantic whispers.

"Oh my!" they exclaimed. "What should we do?!" they cried. "Someone please stop him!"

Dylan had a bad feeling something terrible would happen, and he wasn't wrong. Just as the violent act was about to take place, Anna fearlessly jumped out. Reacting reflexively to her impulsivity,

Dylan rushed out after her with his thoughts centered not on avoiding the giant brute's attack, but on saving her instead. The man's hand had slammed into Dylan's cheek, rattling the brain in his skull and enforcing upon him overwhelming pain.

That was when he passed out.

"My head hurts a bit," Dylan said, returning to the present. "Could you let me rest alone for a while?"

His parents understood that he wanted them to leave the room, and, although reluctant, they acquiesced to his request nonetheless. As soon as he was alone, Dylan buried his head into his pillow, releasing a wretched scream into its fluffy depths.

He must've looked so pathetic back then! Knocked unconscious, and not even because he had been punched. All it took was a slap! Just thinking about it made him feel dreadfully small and pitiful. And, on top of that, his cheek would undoubtedly grow even more swollen come next morning, meaning he would be in no state to be seen by others. He couldn't possibly let Anna see him like this.

If only he could flee the house. He wanted to leave this place and go somewhere far, far away.

❈ ❈ ❈

"Where did Dylan go this time?" Sir Crane asked.

"How should I know?" Madam Jane responded. "It seems like he's still at home... Perhaps he's staying in the library, reading books."

Right on time for their meal, the household's head couple exchanged conversation in the dining room, looking to the empty seat that Dylan was supposed to occupy. After losing consciousness and being brought back home, Dylan had isolated himself. It had been four days since he had last shown his face in the dining room.

"That's good, actually. His face isn't looking too well. In the end, this is better than having him walking about outside."

Anna carried some dishes of food to the table and kept her ears open to listen in on the conversation. She still hadn't thanked Dylan for what he had done for her back in town. Knowing that the house was a huge mansion with plenty of places to be and she was always running around working somewhere in it, she assumed that she would eventually run into him sooner or later, but she hadn't seen him even once.

"Samantha."

"Yes, Madam."

"Please give this medicine to Dylan for me. It's an ointment given to us by someone we should be grateful toward, and they said it's effective for treating bruises." Madam Jane handed Samantha the medicine in question. For some reason, her mood looked rather good today. "Ah, and make sure to confirm that he applies it to his face as well."

Having received the order, Samantha walked out of Madam Jane's line of sight, frowning down at the round container of ointment with annoyance. "Anna, girl," she called.

Anna had gone back to the kitchen, rolling up her sleeves in order to prep herself for washing the dishes later. She looked up as Samantha approached her. Samantha handed her the ointment she received from Madam Jane.

"I have a lot of work to do, so you must attend to Master Dylan in my place," Samantha began. "You heard what the madam had said just then, right? You have to make sure he puts it on his face. Don't just leave after giving it to him." She started pointing, waving her index finger right up to Anna's nose. She spoke firmly as if to drill her commands into Anna's memory.

"Me?" Anna asked.

"Yes, Anna. You. And this is a warning: don't even think about handing your work over to someone else just because you don't want to do it."

Anna adopted a depressed expression. "Understood," she murmured.

Seeing that, Samantha was awash with satisfaction. She felt a huge wave of euphoria knowing that she forced Anna onto an annoying and tedious task.

Anna looked upset upon leaving the kitchen, but her attitude thoroughly shifted once she was completely out. She even lifted her heavy and cumbersome skirt up to ease her way, determination writ plain on her face as she traveled around the mansion in search of Dylan. Now, she didn't need to hold onto those hopes of running into him by

CHRONICLES OF THE KILNER FAMILY

chance. She had a reason to go see him directly.

She started her search by heading over to his room first, but when that proved fruitless, she visited the bathroom, yard, and library. She even searched rooms that were void of occupancy, opening every door to properly check on the rooms' contents. However, no matter how hard she looked, Dylan simply wasn't there. Even Madam Jane's supposition that he would be in the library had been wrong.

"Just where is he?" Anna murmured to herself. She was on the fourth-floor landing and was about to head back down to the lower levels when her eyes fell upon the staircase heading up to the fifth floor. It was the only place she hadn't checked. "No way," she whispered.

The fifth floor of the Kilner family mansion was a deserted place. Everyone, even Madam Jane, avoided it.

When looking at the mansion from the outside, a small window could be spotted on top of its two-pointed rooftops. That window indicated the location of the fifth-floor loft. Anna traveled up the stairs leading there, but it was a place she had never set foot in throughout all three years of her employment.

One of the maids said that when she went up to the fifth floor, she saw a white fog. Another claimed she heard a strange creaking sound despite no one else being near. However, Anna couldn't shake the feeling that this was where Dylan would be, so she didn't turn around to leave.

At the end of the stairs, blocking the way to the rest of the floor, was a door made of wood. When she grabbed the handle and turned, the door opened more smoothly than she assumed it would.

"Master?" Anna called quietly.

She couldn't sense anyone's presence, yet she still summoned her courage and stepped through the threshold. The small room she found within, albeit the source of countless rumors, didn't turn out to be particularly unique or interesting. It had an old bookshelf that didn't have a single book on it, a table, and a sofa that still looked to be in good condition right below a small window. On the sofa lay Dylan, sleeping with his arms acting as pillows.

"Master Dylan," Anna called once more. When her voice escaped her, however, it did so quietly enough that waking him seemed doubtful. She came closer to him, observing him. His left cheek was a swollen purple bruise, still recovering from the hit he had received from the drunk.

The sight wrapped Anna in guilt. As she dealt with her feelings, Dylan, sensing her presence, opened his eyes. As soon as he did, he caught sight of her and quickly rose in surprise.

"H-how did you know about this place?" he asked.

Anna handed him the ointment she was carrying. "The madam had told me to give this to you, so..."

"Leave it here and go," he said bluntly, avoiding eye contact.

"She said that I should at least make sure you put it on your skin. I'll leave after I see you do so."

"It's fine. Just go. There's no mirror here anyways, and—"

"Then I'll apply it for you."

Anna, filled with a sense of duty, kneeled in front of the sofa Dylan was sitting on, determined to get the medicine onto his face no matter what. He was still telling her about how unnecessary it was to do so when she scooped a dollop of ointment onto her fingers, making him fall silent. She was serious about this, he knew then, and there was no use in trying to chase her out now that she had already seen his face.

He gave up on trying to fight against her, but when she came right up to him, saying, "Please excuse me," he started growing even more conscious of her, his primal instincts surging into place. He could feel her breath upon his left, falling upon his cheek and ear, so he turned his face away, trying his best to direct his thoughts elsewhere.

As a result, he didn't notice the look of guilt and pity Anna directed toward his bruise. Seeing such a precious and noble person's face so injured and ruined tore her heart apart. She couldn't understand why Dylan would do such a foolish thing. When she sighed, he turned back toward her.

"Why did you do it?" she asked, putting down the ointment. He looked at her questioningly, still sitting on the sofa with her kneeling before him. "Why did you involve yourself at that moment and allow yourself to end up this way?" she clarified.

Upon hearing her, Dylan smirked coldly. "How laughable."

"No, I'm serious. I didn't say that to make you laugh."

"And if I had chosen not to involve myself?" he asked.

"Then I would've been hit instead," she said. "That would've been better. That way, you wouldn't have ended up in such a terrible state, Young Master."

Her words irritated Dylan because they implied that he should've just watched her get beaten. She was reprimanding him for not behaving cowardly and staying with the crowd, for forgoing the choice that would've left her at the mercy of the drunken man.

"Do you even realize how stupid and foolish the things you're telling me sound right now?" he shouted in anger. "If that's all you wanted to say then just lea—"

Anna interrupted him with a kiss. He fell silent, her mouth sealing his. Her thick, red lips lightly pressed closer before parting to allow them to speak once more.

"I'm sorry. And thank you," she said, but Dylan only narrowed his eyes. "Are you still angry because of what happened that one day?"

"No."

He crossed his arms and leaned back deeply into the sofa. 'Looks like he's still angry,' Anna thought.

"Honestly, I couldn't believe you back then, Master." He didn't respond. "You hated me and tried to chase me out of the household, after all." A pang of guilt struck him. "Yet still, you've saved me from danger twice now."

She began to trust in him. When he protected her from Samantha's vitriol back at the stairs, her heart thumped loudly in her chest, and when she had heard that he took the drunken man's blow in place of her, she had felt the depth of his genuine care for her. He no longer hated her. Anna wanted to convey to him the truth of her feelings as well.

"I wanted to apologize," she said, placing both of her hands atop his thighs. She felt the muscles of his legs contract beneath her palms, tightening into a tense bundle. He was clenching his teeth hard enough the veins of his neck stood in stark relief.

"Are you saying you actually want to apologize, or are you asking for something else?" he asked.

Her hands slid across his thighs and slowly traveled upwards. Her gaze fell upon the tent in his crotch, risen high with the fabric stretched taut across it, binding what lay beneath in place. Then, she lifted her eyes to meet his own and said, "Both."

Dylan kept his arms folded as he gestured with his chin toward her. It was as if she had been given the go-ahead to do whatever she wanted.

Anna bravely placed her hand upon the buckle of his belt. She undid it and then unzipped his pants. After pulling down the thin underwear beneath, his full length sprang out as if it had been waiting for her, tapping the edge of her chin.

After watching her rather pathetic attempts Dylan burst into laughter, but then Anna unflinchingly took hold of his manhood like it was a stick of candy, driving his laughter away. She studied his expression as she began to move her hand up and down his shaft. The way it seemed to throb in her hands felt odd.

His eyebrow twitched. She slowly started to increase the speed of her motions and his face flushed, blushing from the base of his neck to the tip of his ears. Eventually, he uncrossed his arms, grabbing hold of the sofa instead. His dark red lips parted, a slight moan escaping him.

It was unbelievably erotic and wholly seductive. Watching his mouth, she spoke, wondering to herself how he would sound when aroused. "I saw something that looked exactly like this in the streets yesterday."

He bristled. "What?" he asked, brows lifting in surprise.

"When I went to buy some sausages, I thought of how similar they looked. I was reminded of you the moment I saw them, Master." Anna appeared innocent and happy despite the fact that she was essentially admitting to having lascivious thoughts of her master, comparing his shaft to mere sausages.

"Beyond the appearance... the taste. Aren't you curious... about the taste?" Dylan proposed, arousal straining his voice. He sounded like the devil, enticing Anna with wicked deeds.

"I am," she answered without hesitation. She was curious about the taste, but she also wanted to turn him on even more. She wanted to hear him moan, begging for her to continue.

After wetting her dry lips with her tongue, she sank them over his rod, taking it entirely into her mouth before sucking on it and pulling away with a distinct pop. Having felt every ounce of her first taste, Dylan's chest heaved, his breathing becoming increasingly labored. Then, she tilted her head toward him once more and resumed sucking. She slurped and sampled him with her tongue, and just as it looked like she was about to finish cleaning him up, she pulled him deep down her throat.

"Ngh!"

She had given him no warning. His hips stuttered upwards and his head whipped back, hitting the sofa. Meanwhile, Anna started to bob her head up and down his full length, the sound of his harsh panting filling the air. She gripped his thighs tightly and immersed herself in apologizing, in expressing her genuine remorse regarding what happened to him.

Anna could feel him reaching deep down her neck and the sensation instinctively made her want to throw up. At that moment, Dylan pulled out of her and she coughed fitfully as soon as she was free.

"Are you wet?" he asked her. She nodded in assent after her coughing subsided.

He immediately pulled her face toward him for a kiss. As he did so, he laid her down onto the sofa, his hand reaching up her skirt and divesting her of her underwear. He broke the kiss and lifted one of her legs over the back of the sofa. The position bared her to him, revealing the black of her pubic hair and the delicate pink of her heated core.

"You're going too fast," Anna said, embarrassed.

He took his thick shaft in hand and rubbed it against her slit, teasing her. She stretched her arms out toward him, and he leaned into them, showering her lips with an endless litany of kisses. As he rubbed himself against her sensitive flesh, warm, hot precum began to gradually leak out of the tip, moistening his manhood along with her dripping juices. He began to enter her, slipping slowly inside of her.

When he had gone halfway in, he started to slowly rock his hips. Anna sought to match his rhythm. Their hot breaths intermingled and they never broke their shared gaze. He would push himself deeper into her with every thrust, filling her up. As soon as he bottomed out, she gasped aloud, her body jerking against him.

He reached behind her and pulled down the zipper of her dress. Then, he pulled it off her, taking her bra along with it in a single movement. Dylan took a moment to enjoy her nude visage before he resumed thrusting his hips. The sofa, which had already been creaking, started to strain even louder as time went on. The area seemed to grow hot enough to drive anyone away from its exorbitant temperatures. The lewd sound of their bodies meeting, flesh slapping against flesh, resounded throughout the room.

Dylan increased his pace. Anna's breasts swayed to the rhythm of their coupling. He took hold of her soft mounds, spurring his arousal into greater heights. She was shaking beneath him, and instead of holding onto his shoulder, she gripped the sofa, crying out in a combined mixture of pain and ecstasy.

He slammed his entire length into her, reaching as far as he could go, and Anna screamed. Her legs seized and she felt herself fall apart. Dylan, joining her, trembled intensely, collapsing over her. Instead of voicing his climax with a loud moan, he emptied the results of his pleasure into her depths.

Anna's arm slipped off the sofa. She wanted to lift her hand and stroke his back, but she couldn't even muster up the strength for it.

Four

"I told you to buy rosemary, yet this is basil!" Hans exclaimed. He was the head chef of the Kilner household's kitchen and he had been working for the family even longer than Samantha. After having made the unbelievable mistake of sending out an undercooked chicken that one time, he had been on edge for quite a while.

"But Samantha definitely..." Anna began, but Hans was too overcome with rage to listen to her excuse. He turned right around and went back into the kitchen.

"You over there!" he shouted. "Go exchange this with some rosemary and bring it back!"

Samantha definitely told Anna to buy basil. Unfortunately, Anna was incapable of saying anything in her defense, so all she could do was feel dejected as she turned to leave.

Casey found her. "Anna, girl. Master Dylan told you to bring him some chamomile tea."

"Me?"

"Yep. He said that it must be you. Did you make some kind of mistake again?" Casey asked. She looked at Anna with a gaze that conveyed precisely how convinced she was that Anna must've messed up again. She clicked her tongue in pity.

With some chamomile tea prepared on a tray, Anna went up to Dylan's room and knocked on the door. "I've brought the tea you ordered," she announced.

"Come in."

Inside Dylan's room was another servant working hard to change the window's curtains under Samantha's orders. Samantha approached Anna as soon as the latter entered the room.

"Have you finished all your duties before coming here?" she asked.

"Yes. Well, I did, but..."

"What is it?"

"...Nothing," Anna shook her head. "It's nothing at all."

Samantha regarded her curiously, but Anna decided not to mention it. Samantha definitely couldn't have given her the wrong orders on purpose. She was human, after all, and sometimes people just get rosemary and basil confused.

Anna came up to Dylan, glancing at him as he read a book. "Shall I pour the tea?" she asked him. Instead of replying verbally, he slowly nodded just once, remaining focused on his book. She felt a pang of disappointment at his inattentiveness.

She was pouring tea into his cup when the title of the book he was reading strangely caught her attention.

Anna felt that the book looked familiar, and it didn't take her long to realize that it was one of the books David had requested Anna to personally go and buy.

Why would the Master be reading that book? she wondered.

While she was preoccupied with gazing curiously at the book, Dylan reached out and lifted the teapot she was pouring by its spout with a finger. The teacup she was supposed to be filling was full to the brim, nearly spilling over. Surprised, Anna quickly pulled the teapot away and set it down onto the table.

Dylan didn't say anything in particular about her would-be blunder. Although she wanted to stay by his side for a while longer, she was aware she had no real reason to, so she gave him a bow and turned to make her leave. At the same time, the other servant working nearby finished their work on the curtains, having lifted and pulled them off, so they were preparing to leave as well.

Just as Anna was about to open the door, Dylan's voice rang out, driving them all to a halt. "Stop," he said. "I think I ordered a different variety of tea."

No, that wasn't it. He was specifically holding onto Anna so she would have to stay behind with him while the other two left.

A particularly loud sigh came from Samantha, and Anna began to wonder why everything seemed to go wrong today. Why was Master Dylan being so cold and terrible to her now when he was so different yesterday? Her mood hit rock bottom. Rather than the fact that she had messed up twice today, it was his attitude toward her that made her feel worse.

"I apologize. I'll bring some new tea for you," Anna said.

Dylan slid his chair back and stood up. The sound of the motion was audible. His chilling eyes drifted past Anna and toward the other two employees. They got the message quick, leaving the room in fear of being dragged into trouble along with Anna. Soon enough, she stood alone.

"What kind of tea should I bring?" she asked.

They had left the door open behind her. Dylan began to shout as he approached her. "Why do you keep letting your mind wander like this?" he fumed. "Do you even know how many mistakes you've made up until now? Can you honestly not go a single day without making one?"

He slammed the door shut and Anna flinched, frightened by the sound. Yesterday he had kindly held her, personally unzipping her uniform for her, yet now it seemed as if he had returned to his old self, hell-bent on kicking her out of the household.

Anna could barely keep her tears in check, genuine concern creeping into her voice. "Master, why are you treating me like this?"

"You really don't know?" The look in his eyes was serious.

She pouted, wholeheartedly upset. "Yes," she said. "I don't understand, so please explain."

Dylan began to stroke her lower lip. Anna must have given her all in serving him yesterday for her lips had swollen overnight. It didn't seem like she realized just how seductive the sight of it looked to him.

"It's so I could do this," he said, clasping their mouths together in a kiss. It was deep and passionate, lifting Anna's heavy, rock-bottom heart slowly back up.

He intentionally kicked them out. For this.

Parting, Dylan gave Anna's forehead a quick peck. "I have something to give you personally as well, after all."

"Something to give me?"

He guided her to a chair in front of a glass round table. Then, he pulled a rectangular box out of hiding from under his bed, presenting it to her. He kneeled down before her, and she shifted in place, uncomfortable with the gesture. He seemed unfazed by it, however, instead pulling out a black shoe from within the box.

He took the old, worn shoes Anna was wearing off for her. "I can at least buy my own shoes, you know," she said. These new shoes may have been the cheapest ones for sale in the shop, but Anna still regarded them hesitantly, burdened by his generosity.

"I didn't buy it so you don't need to worry about it."

"You didn't? Then who did?"

"I got it for free after buying a different pair of shoes. I only took the offer since they seemed to be the perfect size for your feet," he explained.

"Really?"

Hearing this, Anna's expression became a little lighter. After Dylan slipped the shoes onto her, she turned them about, admiring them from every angle she could manage. Standing up, she spun around, her voice rising in pitch with her elation.

"My goodness, they fit me perfectly!" she exclaimed. Dylan cracked a smile, nodding his head.

"I thought so," he said. "That's why I'm giving them to you."

Seeing her so happy made him feel happy as well. Certain that she wouldn't have another unfortunate accident involving stepping on anything dangerous—like glass, perhaps—while wearing those flimsy old shoes, some of his worries began to fade.

"I don't know who gave these to you for free, but please thank them for me."

Suddenly, Dylan's joy fled him and irritation took its place. "Although someone else gave them to me, it was I who gave them to you."

"So what you mean by that is that if someone hadn't handed them to you for free, I wouldn't be wearing them right now, huh?"

"No, I mean...!"

"*Pfft!*" Anna grabbed her stomach, laughing from deep within her belly.

Dylan understood, then, that he had played right into her hand. Nevertheless, seeing her laugh in such a way made him laugh too, and he forgot his anger.

✳ ✳ ✳

"Samantha," Dylan called.

"Yes, Master?"

"I'm planning to make use of the fifth-floor loft."

Samantha waited patiently for Dylan to continue speaking, expecting more to the sentence, but then she realized what he was actually asking for. She nodded vigorously. "Oh, I understand," she said. "I'll make sure to clean up the loft for you immediately."

She promptly turned around, intending to carry out the task, but then Dylan quickly intervened. "Wait!" he cried.

He objected so fast it looked suspicious.

"The loft has tons of dust. Numerous cobwebs

in every corner. And, in any case, you'll need things to fill up the room with as well, and..."

Samantha couldn't understand what Dylan was trying to say in the slightest. It didn't befit him. He was usually the type to converse without any hesitation in his voice. However, the way he spoke now was hesitant and his sentences ran awkwardly long. He kept delaying what he truly intended to convey. It was making Samantha annoyed.

"So what I'm saying is... since it'll be tough work, you should try sending someone in particular. A servant that keeps making excuses and always messes up on the job."

Aware that all he needed to say in the first place was 'send Anna up there,' Dylan was peeved at himself for hesitating so much.

"That's a great idea," Samantha said, smiling brightly after finally picking up on what Dylan was trying to say. "I know a girl that'll be perfect for this."

As soon as she heard Dylan's description, Anna came to mind, popping up instantly. After Samantha started hating her, every little thing she did seemed to grate on Samantha's mind. Master David, who usually protected Anna, wasn't present in the mansion. However, Master Dylan, who shared Samantha's sentiments and actively hated Anna, would be with her in the loft, so Samantha had no reason to object to the command. "I'll send that child to the loft immediately," she said.

"No!" Once again, Dylan stopped her. "First, I

need to pick out some things to put up there."

"Ah, I see." Samantha's expression conveyed a sense of understanding. She fixed up her dress. "Then, I'll aid you as you pick them out."

Why is she being so slow? Why isn't she getting my hints? Dylan wondered, exasperated. He couldn't help frowning, his forehead creasing. "No, I'll be going with the girl for this as well. Because... because there'll be tons of things to bring."

✳ ✳ ✳

The mansion's giant front doors began to open, revealing Anna as she stepped past them. Dylan exhaled a relieved sigh, allowing himself a small smile.

"Walk beside me," he said.

They left the area and walked toward a place where people working inside the mansion couldn't see them. It was only then that Dylan turned back around to face her.

"I'm more comfortable walking behind you, Master," Anna said.

"Is that so? Then maybe I'll try walking behind you this time."

Stopping his stride, Dylan waited for Anna to pass him. She looked around and shook her head, but he continued to request it of her, eventually driving her to relent. She walked in front of him and he trailed after her.

Her hair was bundled up into a cute bun. Her long, slender neckline and the gentle slope of her shoulders looked beautiful. Even the way her skirt swayed gently up and down with the rhythm of her footsteps seduced him. He couldn't take his eyes off her.

"Didn't you say there were things that you needed?" Anna asked. "If you mean to visit the shops, we're going in the opposite direction right now."

"I know," Dylan replied.

"Then where are we going right now?"

"Well, I'm not really sure about that, either."

"Huh?"

She stared at Dylan, and her eyes seemed to ask, *If you don't know either, then why are we doing this?*

Before she could register it, however, Dylan came up to her and took her hand in his, interlocking their fingers. "It's not like we can only ever take walks when we have a clear goal," he said.

The two of them matched their strides, traveling across a dense forest together. Eventually, they reached the forest's end, a place where the shade began to dwindle and the land gave way to a field of short grass. Amongst the field was a calm lake whose depth remained indecipherable.

"So there was a lake here!" Anna exclaimed.

"You're right. There really is."

"The way the setting sun scatters its beams across the waters of the lake is gorgeous."

Anna couldn't look away from the lake's sparkling colors. Dylan, meanwhile, couldn't look away from Anna. Her eyes sparkled even more wondrously than the lake which captured her gaze.

"It's beautiful."

"Yes, it really is."

They walked around the lake in silence for a long time. Dylan was jealous of the lake and how it stole Anna's attention away from him, but since he didn't want to ruin all the fun she was having, he kept his mouth shut, staying quietly by her side.

However, despite his considerate efforts, the clouds took to covering the sun. They prevented it from shining down upon the lake any further as if intentionally denying Anna her enjoyment.

"The clouds look ominous," Dylan said, squinting as he looked to the sky.

Black clouds started to coalesce across the sky, making it almost impossible to believe that the weather had been clear just a few moments ago.

"We should return quickly," Anna said, turning around to head back where they came.

Dylan grabbed her hand. "It's already too late," he meant to say, but before he could even finish speaking, a long, lengthy raindrop landed right on Anna's forehead.

Their gazes met. Then, at the same time, they both walked toward the direction they came from.

Although it was bad that the rain was harsh enough to disturb their vision, they inevitably couldn't imagine running all the way back home with it pummeling them as heavily as it had now begun to.

"What do we do now?" Anna asked. Her voice was washed out by the rain, and she wasn't sure if Dylan had gotten her message.

He surveyed their surroundings. Then, he spotted a small house deeper into the forest. "Let's go in there first," he said, "so we can get out of the rain." He took her hand once more and they broke into a sprint.

Huff... huff.

Stopping in front of the modest wooden hut, they collected their breath. Before he started knocking on the door, Dylan instinctively directed Anna behind him so he could shield her presence with his. He had to bend down a bit due to the door's unusually low height.

"Is anyone there?" he called. There came no answer. After knocking one more time only to receive the same result, Dylan went ahead and carefully turned the doorknob, discovering that it was never locked. He made sure to check that no one was inside before he brought Anna in.

Judging from the old fishing rod leaning on the wall, the place seemed to serve as temporary housing for people who wished to rest and recuperate. It was a small and convenient home offering only a few chairs and a small pot stove.

The pair's body temperatures were falling drastically in the aftermath of getting soaked by the rain. Upon noticing Anna's complexion rapidly draining into a pallor, Dylan hurriedly lit up the stove. "It would be best to take off your clothes," he said.

"What if someone comes in?"

"There's no one who would willingly come all the way out here in this kind of weather."

Anna's expression still conveyed some skepticism despite his claim as to the impossibility of anyone finding them. Turning to the window, she wiped the condensation from the glass and peered outside to check on the weather. However, due to how heavy the rain had become, she couldn't see anything beyond her position inside.

Dylan was right. The only people crazy enough to endure this kind of weather and come all the way here were him and herself.

He removed his shirts and pants first, laying them on the back of a chair and revealing his prominent musculature and rock-hard abs as he strutted around the hut. Anna followed his lead and pulled down the zipper on her back, taking off her dress and brassiere so she could hang them on the back of a chair as well.

Keeping her chest concealed with her hands wrapped tight around her arms, she sat before the stove and tried to get warm.

"Looks like this is the only thing that will be useful," Dylan announced, procuring a blanket from somewhere and draping it over Anna's shoulder. He sat down right next to her.

"Wouldn't other people be worried about us?" Anna asked.

Dylan easily addressed her worries and reassured her. "They'll probably think we're off avoiding the rain somewhere."

The embers on the stove seemed to flare for a moment. The warm glow of the fire spread itself gently across the couple's bare skin.

"It looks like I only ended up troubling you by bringing you all the way out here," he murmured, depressed.

Anna shook her head and locked her arms around his. He could feel her perky, bouncy breasts squishing against his muscular arm. "I'm plenty happy. I got to know about this beautiful place. If I died without knowing this place ever existed, I would have regretted it for all eternity."

"Do you speak honestly?"

"Yes. There isn't a single lie in anything I've said."

She looked up at him and smiled, her beautiful white teeth glistening. He turned his head to glance down at her and as he did so, he felt himself offer her a smile of his own.

A moment of silence passed.

Every passing sensation between them drew their attention, the rub of their bare skin against each other becoming the height of their focus with every slight shift. Dylan's arm was pressed securely against Anna's breasts by now, and if he moved even the smallest inch, he could feel their softness, the draw of her erect nipples upon his flesh. It was obvious she was enjoying this situation as well.

Every ounce of contact brought forth dangerous

heights of tension. Hot embers began to smolder within Dylan, burning as hot as the flames within the stove before them.

"Climb on top of me," he said, breaking the silence. Turning, Anna directed her wide-eyed gaze toward him. "Now!" he said, pressuring her as if she were a small child.

Her eyelashes trembled as she compiled and released the blanket that lay over her shoulders. It tumbled to the ground, revealing her figure, and he couldn't take his eyes off of her beautiful silhouette, accentuated by the shadows in the room. She was staring down at him, capturing his gaze within her own as she lowered herself to sit on top of him with her legs spread apart.

He placed his hands behind her knees and pulled her closer to him. As he did so, his erect manhood slid against the fabric of her thin underwear.

"*Nnh...*" Anna shivered, a small moan escaping her. The motion made her breasts bounce up and down as if to seduce him.

He showered numerous kisses atop her collarbone. "Let me bite them," he whispered.

Even without providing a detailed explanation, Anna understood what he meant because he licked his lips and stared hungrily at her round, plump bosom. She took her breasts in both hands as the soft flesh proved too ample to hold in a single one and, with a gulp, guided it between Dylan's lips. His tongue was hot and serpentine. He licked her nipple then carefully began to suck on it like a child, the whole of her petite, pink areola clasped beneath his mouth.

Anna let out a moan, feeling tickled. She held the back of Dylan's head with her right hand as he suckled on one breast while her left was squeezing the other as if to coax milk out of it. Trapped within his mouth, her nipple was subject to an onslaught of nibbling, pressing, and biting. Anna responded fervently to the ecstasy he provided.

Then, he brought his attention over to her other breast, taking it between his lips. As he did so, he took hold of the nipple he had moistened, trapping it between his index finger and thumb before squeezing.

"*Aah!*"

Anna's breathing grew labored. She ground her hips against Dylan, who, judging by the large bulge rubbing against her underwear, seemed just as aroused as she was. His free hand, which stood planted upon her hips, tightened their grip.

"Go ahead. Move however you want," he said, laying himself down upon the blanket.

Anna placed her hands upon his hard chest to balance herself then slowly moved her butt to grind further against his erection. His lips parted seductively, a moan akin to a whisper drifting from him and dripping with satisfaction. Feeling confident, she became even braver with her movements, gyrating her hips and ushering herself back and forth atop him. The resulting friction inspired vivid sensations, almost as if his manhood had breached her underwear and found its way inside.

She bit her lip, but it wasn't enough to suppress the mounting arousal coursing through her body. As if she were dying, she groaned loudly through her clenched teeth.

Suddenly, Dylan took hold of her legs. It was like she was a boat departing its port and he meant to anchor her. "Now... stop."

Anna didn't have much endurance. He didn't want her to reach climax alone when they weren't in a proper position yet.

She lowered her head and kissed him deeply. His hand slid up her back and with a single quick, elegant movement, he set her upon the blanket he was lying on. He never stopped kissing her.

"*Haah... haah...*"

She waited for him to fill her up inside with half-lidded eyes. Pulling her underwear down, he positioned himself between her legs.

"Are you ready?" he asked. His voice was a tone lower. Anyone hearing it would shiver with excitement and anticipation. Anna nodded hurriedly in response.

As soon as she gave the signal, he took hold of his length. It looked swollen enough to explode from all the pressure, pushing through the black forest between her thighs and rubbing against her soft and supple bud.

"*Nngh!*"

He could see Anna curl her hand into a fist. She was already wet enough to take all of him inside her.

"Hold onto your legs," he instructed softly. She grabbed the back of her knees, folding herself in half. Then, Dylan pushed further between her legs and stuck half of his rod inside her. They both shouted at the same time, a scream composed of equal parts pain and delight.

Dylan didn't try to rush. He made sure to move slowly and carefully so that she could get used to him. Gradually, her body began to heat up, making her beg for more. He nibbled on her earlobe with his pristine white teeth, licking into her ear, making her inner muscles clench even tighter around his throbbing length. With it halfway inside of her, he rolled his hips in a circular motion. In response, Anna pulled their hips closer together, bringing him right up to her as if the blanket underneath her would rip.

"*A-ah…!*"

His smooth motions, as calm as a lake, suddenly grew rough like the churning waves of the sea crashing against the rocks. Suddenly immersed in this unexpected sensation, Anna's body seized, shaking like a freshly caught fish. Every time he thrust himself forward, she would respond to the action by pushing herself along with him and feeling his manhood reach deeper inside her.

Dylan kept his eyes locked onto hers as he filled her over and over again.

"Deeper! Deeper...!" Anna yelled, begging for it.

"Bend over."

Her arms, now holding her body up, shivered

weakly. Her knees settled on the ground and her upper body arched up. He grabbed her round bottom and pushed his member deep inside her. At that moment, Anna lost all the remaining strength she had in her arms and she collapsed onto the floor, her hips the only part of her remaining aloft by Dylan's grasp.

He paid her fall no mind. He kept thrusting into her, reaching even deeper until he filled her with him completely. Every time he moved, Anna weakly moaned aloud, but soon enough, she began to match his rhythm, meeting every swing of his hips. She squeezed down hard on the fleshy rod within her before letting go again. The sound of their flesh slapping against each other resounded in the small hut, Anna's butt growing redder in color as time went on and their bodies continued to collide.

"*Ahh...!*"

Dylan lowered his torso until it remained flush against her back, pressing his powerful body into hers. An unfamiliar sensation began to swirl around within her and for a moment she believed she would be crushed underneath him.

"Not yet," he said.

However, his manhood still maintained its vicious temper, threatening her passionately. He hoisted her up and soon enough, Anna's breasts, once gripped by Dylan's hands, were squished against the cold window. It was still raining outside.

Dylan pummeled into her from behind, positioned right between her spread legs. Their heated breaths manifested as fog in the crisp air. Every time she twisted her hips slightly, she would feel him stab a side within her she never could've expected and tremors would rock her bottom as a haunting moan escaped her.

Dylan's glutes tensed hard, contending with the strain of maintaining the speed of his powerful thrusts. He displayed his thirst for Anna's love with increasing passion and aggression.

As the both of them writhed, panting roughly, her lips slowly parted.

Rumble. Crack!

Thunder broke through the sky.

Right at that moment, she screamed as if she had been struck by lightning. Looking as if she would faint, her body wavered tremulously. Something hot began to dribble between her legs.

Dylan's hand slapped against the window's white frosted glass and left an imprint in the condensation. He kissed Anna's forehead and began to whisper.

"No matter what anyone says from now on, you are my woman."

✳ ✳ ✳

"The rain has gotten heavier. I hope nothing bad happened to them... should I send out some people?" Madam Jane fretted, pacing around a large window with a red curtain hanging upon it. The rain had started in the afternoon and it had been pouring endlessly ever since.

"We're getting anxious because you won't calm down about this," Sir Crane said. "They'll return safe and unharmed so please just sit down and wait for them."

Taking his words into account, Madam Jane obliged and sat down on the sofa. The family had gathered to sit down in the living room for the first time in a good while to wait for David and his wife to return from their trip. They were scheduled to arrive soon.

"You were hit heavily by the rain a few days ago, weren't you, Dylan? Are you feeling unwell?" Madam Jane asked, her voice tinged with concern. Once he came into view, she noticed that he had kept quiet the entire time, seemingly deep in thought.

Dylan simply shook his head. "No, I'm just worried about them, too."

Upon receiving his answer, Madam Jane turned to Sir Crane as if to ask, 'You feel the same, don't you?'

However, Dylan's thoughts were of a completely different variety.

He hadn't understood why, ever since a few days ago, he had become so sleepless and riddled with indigestion. Even though he took Anna into his embrace and confirmed, once and for all, that she was his woman from then on, he still felt anxious. He was wondering what could possibly be making him feel like this when he realized, just yesterday, that David and Carol's trip would soon come to an end.

Casey hurriedly ran in, yelling, "Master David has returned!"

Madam Jane shot up from her seat with a bright grin. Seeing her rise in such a way made Sir Crane click his tongue in mild annoyance. Dylan followed behind his parents as they left, his mind on Anna and how she was probably working elsewhere in the mansion.

"Did you have a good trip?" Madam Jane asked, greeting David and Carol intensely. It had been a month since she last saw them, after all. "Is Sir Adams still good and healthy?"

Carol answered with a smile. "Yes, we had a great trip thanks to you two. Father, Mother, we're glad to see that both of you are still doing well," she said. Although she had spent the month before her departure looking depressed and terribly weak, she looked brighter after visiting her original parents.

Madam Jane took Carol's hands and gushed. "That's great news."

"I'm sure the trip here was a long one," Sir Crane said. "It must have been hard on you, so how about we cut the greetings here and have a meal?"

If Sir Crane didn't gracefully intervene, Madam Jane would have kept going. David and Carol's welcome would've continued for way too long, leaving all of them standing by the front entrance.

Thankfully, Madam Jane didn't notice Sir Crane's intentions. She began guiding the two into the house since they were probably hungry by now. "Yes, your father is right. Let's get your stomachs filled up first."

"I'm not actually hungry at the moment, but she is," David said, indicating Carol. "Since we were rattling around in that carriage the whole time, my stomach isn't feeling very well. I'm afraid I'll have to retire to my room."

"Huh? I-I see. That can happen, of course. It must've been terrible for you since it rained all day and everything. Go ahead and rest in your room."

Without sparing Carol even a single glance, David gave her the cold shoulder and ascended the stairs to his quarters. Madam Jane studied Carol's reaction, noticing the uneasy tension flowing between them. Their relationship was already on thin ice. They were never seen close to each other, and on top of that, there has been no news of them receiving a child in over three years while other couples were having plenty of their own.

The reason why Madam Jane recommended they go visit Carol's parents in the first place was in the hopes that the trip would help mend their relationship as husband and wife. There was a saying that a couple could develop some new love and affection for each other if they went on a trip and stayed together for a decent amount of time, after all.

However, Madam Jane didn't know the truth. Sometimes trips can end up making relationships worse.

"Are you not hungry, sister-in-law?" Dylan

asked Carol, seeing as she had been left alone.

"No, I'm fine," she answered. "I'm not hungry either, so I was hoping to dine later. Thank you again for your consideration, Mother." She smiled warmly, then followed David up the stairs.

The remaining family members, left behind beyond the staircase, were unsure if they should worry about David's terrible attitude or if they should rejoice in the fact that Carol seemed to have regained her smile.

※ ※ ※

Knock knock.

Dylan rapped on the door to David's personal study. He assumed that David would still be inside of it as opposed to the bedroom he shared with Carol. His assumption was correct.

"Who is it?" David's voice called out.

"It's me, Brother," Dylan answered.

"Come in."

David stood by a desk placed next to the window. He had his back facing Dylan and he was divesting himself of his thick coat, depositing it on a coat rack. In the meantime, Dylan walked up to the desk and placed the book he brought with him down upon its surface.

David turned around and lifted the book up. "What is this?" he asked.

Despite asking, however, he soon realized without much difficulty that it was the book he had requested Anna to buy. He lifted his head and the confused expression upon his face seemed to ask, 'Why do you have this?'

"Since it was a book you had personally ordered, I got curious. I read it first," Dylan said. He studied David's expression carefully. It had softened into the same considerate and kind expression as it had once before, his lips curving into a smile.

"And did that child read it as well?"

It was obvious that the child David was referring to was Anna. Dylan felt a tinge of anger at how clear the connection seemed to be. Knowing that the smile blossoming upon his brother's lips was inspired by her made an unsightly degree of jealousy boil up within him.

Since Dylan didn't answer immediately, David asked once more. "I'm talking about Anna. The girl who bought the book."

Finally. Her name escaped his mouth.

The worry, envy, jealousy, and fear converging inside Dylan's mind made him feel like being petty. "I wonder. I'm not actually sure."

"So, you cheated, didn't you Dylan? Even though I gave that child the right to read that book before anyone else."

The word 'cheated' cut through Dylan's heart like a knife. "'Cheated', you say," he echoed, voice cold. His eyes looked severe; his gaze sharpened to a freezing point. It seemed sharp enough to cut the desk before him into two separate pieces.

I didn't steal Anna from you, Older Brother. She came to me instead, he thought. His hand clenched into a fist, bringing his veins into stark relief. It wasn't cheating. No matter how much David chose to abuse and damage him with those underhanded words, their relationship could never return to how it was once before.

Even if he did cheat, he had no reason to worry. In the end, the one who has conquered Anna had been him, after all.

"Did something happen between you two?" David asked, looking at Dylan with worry. He studied him carefully, since, for some reason, Dylan seemed angry.

Knock knock.

At that moment, someone knocked on the study door. David and Dylan both whipped their heads in that direction at the same time, spotting Carol standing beside the open door. David's countenance grew stiff at the sight of her.

He put a hand on Dylan's shoulder as he spoke. "I'm sorry, but you'll have to leave the room for now."

Dylan obliged. Standing outside of David's personal study, he rubbed at his face with his large hands. Since he hadn't left the area, he could hear them within the study room. Their voices kept rising in anger as they began to argue.

Their relationship had already been on its last legs this entire time, so Dylan didn't understand why he felt so nervous. So worried.

That night, Dylan called Anna up to the fifth-floor loft. The excuse he gave to Samantha stated that he wanted to start cleaning the place up since the process had yet to begin.

However, the girl that arrived to aid him wasn't Anna. Through the girl, Samantha informed him that Anna was predisposed, already tasked with organizing Master David's study. A replacement had been sent in her place.

Dylan wanted to run to his brother's study and immediately drag Anna out by her arm. Instead, he told her replacement to come back later, sending the girl away.

He lied down on the sofa where he and Anna had once climaxed together, his thoughts burdened by his imagination. Anna and his older brother could be alone in the study by now, doing something he had no choice but to remain ignorant of.

It filled Dylan with desolate pain.

✳ ✳ ✳

As soon as Anna began to scrub the windowsill with a washcloth, Dylan grabbed her hand, making her sit down on the sofa.

"I have to clean the room," she protested. "You called me to do that."

"I brought you here so we could spend time together."

"But Samantha thinks I came here to clean instead. She'll definitely come to check if the room's clean or not later. I still have to do my job."

She swatted Dylan's hand away and stood up once more. Regardless of how much he pouted, there was no use. Samantha had been even more aggressive with her attacks against Anna lately. Earlier today she had been following Samantha's orders to put away the curtain hanging in Madam Jane's room and place it in storage. Instead, she got into trouble.

The curtain was something that Madam Jane held dear since it had been hand-made by her mother. Seeing as Anna had suddenly taken it away without any warning, the whole household had been up in arms for a few moments. Madam Jane had only calmed down after taking the curtain back from Anna. Samantha asked for forgiveness in place of Anna, citing that Anna made serious mistakes like that all the time.

Samantha harassed Anna in numerous similar ways, each of them petty and childish. However, no one would believe Anna when she told them that she was simply following Samantha's orders. Samantha was recognized as a talented employee by the Kilner household, working for them for many years, whilst Anna had only started working for them three years ago. Compared to her, Anna was a complete rookie as a maid.

"That book," Dylan began.

"Book?" Anna had moved on to cleaning an empty bookshelf. She glanced toward where Dylan was still sitting on the sofa.

"The book that my older brother requested of

you," he clarified.

"Ah, that book! Oh, dear. Did you return it back to him yourself, Master Dylan?"

"Yeah, I brought it to him myself. But, in any case, that book. Why did my brother order you to buy that particular book?"

Anna's expression turned smug. "He's been making me buy books for the past three years now. It's because I know how to read, after all."

"It's not like there isn't anyone else in this household that can read... so, what I'm asking is: why did it have to be you specifically?" Dylan's forehead creased as he spoke, frowning. In comparison to how seriously Dylan was taking this, Anna looked far too relaxed.

"Madam Jane only ever brings Amy along whenever she goes out to buy tea. Amy knows quite a lot about tea, after all. For example, tea with dried rosemary helps with digestion after meals, and chamomile helps with sleep," Anna explained. She pulled out a new washcloth from an iron washing bucket. "So I think Master David's doing something similar to that. Of course, I wouldn't dare insinuate that my knowledge is on par with his. He's simply being generous to me since he knows that reading is my hobby and he wanted to allow me the opportunity to read more. He's a kind person, after all."

"Yeah," Dylan said. "Kind indeed."

She was right. His older brother was a kind person. However, Dylan was suspicious as to whether this was actually true or not, since, in his eyes, David had been treating Carol terribly this whole time. And the reason as to why might have been because of Anna herself.

"Just like how Madam Jane and Amy connect through tea, I could say that Master David and I connect through books."

What? Dylan's expression grew stiff. "Then, what about me and you?" he asked.

"Huh?" Anna turned her head. She hadn't noticed until now, but he had approached her and he was now right behind her.

"What do you and I connect with?"

At that, she smiled sheepishly in embarrassment. His hands took hold of her hips. Lowering his head, he pressed a collection of kisses along the nape of her neck.

"Jeez," she whined. "I said I can't do it today." She pulled his hands off her and slid herself away from his grip. Dylan's expression grew noticeably dark at the action, but she didn't notice.

"I can give Samantha an excuse for you."

"But, still. We can't."

After getting rejected again, Dylan began to complain, his tone demonstrating his annoyance. "Is there perhaps another reason why then?" he asked testily.

Anna shook her head more intensely than necessary, looking as if she was burdened by some kind of guilt.

Dylan moved over to the windowsill and began to lean on it. His mood didn't look particularly good that day. Later on, he didn't glance at her even once. He kept his gaze directed to the window in anger as if he meant to broadcast how he refused to forgive her.

Anna shrugged her shoulders. She was the only one between them who had to deal with having a period every month, anyway, so she didn't understand why he was being so sensitive.

Five

"Hey, Anna! Anna!"

A middle-aged woman was hurriedly calling out the name of the girl who had run out of the house. However, the girl had already disappeared from sight, running as fast as she could.

Huff! Huff!

Anna ran tirelessly, heedless of the direction she headed toward. She had yet to shed the baby fat from her face, yet she was sprinting desperately, with both of her cheeks wet with an unending flood of tears.

Her dress, handed down from her grandmother from the grandmother before hers, was originally white, but it had faded into a yellowish hue over time. She used the sleeve to wipe away her tears.

Blinded by the motion, she couldn't see the tree root sticking out of the ground before her, so she ended up snagging her foot on it and falling over into a pile of dead leaves.

"*Argh!*" she exclaimed. She moaned in pain as she lay sprawled upon the ground.

It was all so unfair. Her grandfather's words, telling her that bad things always seemed to happen all at once, came to mind. Maybe it was true. That morning, she had dropped all six eggs she received from Mrs. Ann and broke them because of her next-door neighbor, Sebastian's, prank. No matter how many times she explained to her mom that they broke because of Sebastian, her mother still raised a cane against her in punishment.

She was already depressed after realizing all of her mother's love had been stolen by her younger sibling, but then her mother began to whip her re-peatedly, making her wonder if she was just an adopted child or something.

When her dad came back home drunk that night, she had been sobbing into her pillow. Her mother yelled at him, asking him how he managed to drink when their family had no money. He said he picked some money up off the streets, but her mother didn't believe him.

After a long, persistent interrogation, her father

finally revealed the truth: he had sold Button at the market. Hearing the news, Anna ripped off her blanket and bolted right up. She couldn't believe it.

Button was her dog. She had brought him home.

Her mother, catching sight of her shocked expression, slapped her father in the back hard enough that proved audible, but Anna knew that her mother must've been secretly pleased. She had always disliked Button, because the dog did nothing but eat into the household's finances. It was just a small dog, but it still needed feeding, and food wasn't free.

Anna had confronted her parents and yelled, "I'm sure that in the future you'll say that I don't do anything but cost the family money, either! You'll sell me at the market, too!"

She no longer wanted to see her mother's face again. Doubly so for her father. If she found Button again, she would consider going back, but until then, she swore never to return.

The time she had spent with Button may have been short in the end, but to her, Button was more than just a simple pet dog.

"Why did this happen to me?! What did I do wrong?!" she shouted. The more she thought about it, the sadder her situation became. She tried to assuage her tears, but she couldn't keep them from falling, and they poured from her eyes once more. Anna cried until she had nothing left to cry with.

Then, she realized that one of her shoes was missing.

If Anna told her mother that she lost her shoe, she knew she'd get whipped again. Knowing that she had to find it, she lifted herself up and surveyed her surroundings.

"Doesn't... matter," she muttered, her speech becoming halting amidst her sobs. "I won't be going... back home anyways."

Despite what she told herself, however, Anna shuffled toward her lost shoe as soon as she spotted it rolling beside a tree root. She picked it up and cradled it safely in her arms.

At that moment, an unfamiliar man came into view. He was leaning against the tree before her and staring directly at her. Startled at the sight of him, she dropped her shoe.

This was Anna and Dylan's first meeting.

"Have you finished crying?" he asked. Ironically, he, too, had eyes rimmed red, made wet with a trace of tears. In response to his inquiry, Anna nodded in reflex before she caught herself and instead began to shake her head vigorously.

"N-no, I didn't cry," she denied. "I didn't cry at all." She felt embarrassed for having wept like a child.

He smirked. "Then, if not tears, what's that hanging from the corner of your eyes?"

The pungent scent of alcohol filtered from him. It seemed like he had been drinking. Two empty bottles sat upon the ground next to him, confirming Anna's hunch. Her mother told her that the best course of action to take when nearing a drunken man was to avoid them first and foremost. She forced her foot into her discarded shoe and hurriedly searched for an opportunity to run from him as soon as she could.

"The world is sometimes like that," he continued, unprompted. "Sometimes it would present you with an unbelievable amount of happiness, while other times it would force you to embrace such a deep well of sorrow you'd find it difficult to keep on living."

Anna stopped, watching his downcast profile. It seemed like something unfortunate had happened to him recently. Perhaps even something as saddening as what she had just experienced. Her head, once filled with thoughts of escaping him, was now filled with sympathy and a sense of kinship. She didn't know why, but she nevertheless pitied the man before her.

"But, you know, there's nothing in this world you can't endure," he said resolutely. She wasn't sure if he was offering her advice or just speaking aloud as he tried to console himself, heart heavy after exhausting himself by drinking. "You just have to endure it all. No matter what. Then, one day you'd look back and that sadness you once believed insurmountable would seem far away as if it were a dream, and happiness would find you once more. Something will help you get there. It could be time or another person. Or, it could even be something else unspecified."

He looked up, staring into the empty sky. At

that moment, Anna finally spoke. "Button was sold at the market," she mumbled woefully. Dylan turned to her, tilting his head.

"Who was Button?"

"A member of my family. Button was a sibling, a friend, and... even though I had just begun to take a liking to..." Anna trailed off, her round eyes swelling with tears once more.

"Oh dear," he whispered. His eyebrows creased with pity.

"Father said he did it because he needed the money, but can you believe it? Would you sell off your family members for just a few dollars? I'll never be able to understand his actions."

Dylan quietly observed her for a moment. Then, he slipped his hand into his coat pocket, looking for something. He eventually pulled out a key that was as large as two fingers and presented it to her. "Take this," he said. "Go to the Kilner family mansion and ask for a job. My name is Dylan. If you tell them Dylan told you to come by, they'll hire you. And... do you perhaps know the price Button was sold for?"

Anna took the key that Dylan handed over and shook her head in response to his question. At that, he loosened an expensive-looking watch on his wrist and presented it to her. She gawked at it as he placed it into her hand.

"Trade this for Button. Get them back and then come back here."

"But..."

"I'm not just straight-up giving this to you. I'm letting you borrow it," he clarified. Bearing the most merciful expression in the world, he stood up from his seat on the ground, wobbling as he did so. Anna rose as well, following him. "Soon it'll be dark, so go back home. It's not my position to say so, but your family must be worried about you. And you need to bring Button back home, too, right?"

Anna began to sob as she nodded in assent. She wasn't crying due to grief anymore. Instead, she was relieved, the thought that she could reunite with Button bringing tears to her eyes.

Dylan chuckled and patted her on the head a couple times.

"See. I told you that something would come and help you endure in the end."

✱ ✱ ✱

Knock.

Someone tapped concisely on the library door.

"Come in," David answered.

Anna peeked from behind the door like a little rabbit. He knew it was her without even having to lift his head because he had specifically called for her to come by. She walked in, stopping a good distance away from the table he was sitting at.

"Is there something you wanted to request of me?" she asked.

He stopped as he was flipping over a page and

lifted his head to look at her. Glancing up from below his glasses, his eyes met hers and she smiled awkwardly. "I wanted to have a chat since it's been a while," he said, "but since you asked, I have to order you to do something now." Disappointment thickly laced every word.

"No, that's not why I..."

"It feels like, during my month-long absence from this household, the distance between us has grown by six—no, by eight feet further apart than it once was before. Did something happen?" David asked, his voice gentling into a kind, brotherly tone.

Anna kept her mouth shut as she fidgeted. Her mind was preoccupied with concerns, wondering if he could still look at her with eyes as warm as they were now if he heard about the rumors floating around on the streets. Would he blame her for getting him involved in such vulgar gossip?

"Did you hear about a rumor or something?"

She kept her gaze directed downward and shook her head.

"Then I guess there could only be one reason why you're acting like this," he said. Hearing him speak so confidently, fear seized her heart. She lifted her head slightly and as she did so, David began to act strangely, sticking his nose into his arms and sniffing himself. "It's because I smell terrible, isn't it? That's why you're standing so far away."

"N-no, that's definitely not it at all," Anna protested, shaking her head once more and frantically waving her hands in front of her.

David, who had looked completely serious the entire time, now began to smile. Seeing his demeanor shift, she realized he was intentionally saying things just to tease her. It occurred to her how quick she was to scramble to deny his claims just a second ago and she couldn't help but giggle.

"Finally, you're laughing. Now that's the Anna I know," David said. His voice was deep, yet gentle. "I won't ask what had happened or what kind of thoughts you've had that drove you to start staying so far away from me, but if you still love books dearly, and if you don't mind chatting with me, then you can always come by whenever you'd like. Just like how it's always been."

He must have been a saint in the past. Otherwise, there would be no way he'd be able to convey such touching sentiments so honestly.

"We're still managing to converse quite well despite this distance between us, after all."

Anna nodded in agreement. Master David was someone who would comfort her when faced with terrible rumors rather than push her away in disgust. However, it was because of this that she had kept such a distance between them. She knew he was someone that would willingly take the brunt of the damage unjust rumors would bring.

David eventually told her it was fine for her to leave. Exiting the library, she closed the door behind her.

However, on the other side of the door, opposite the entrance to the library, stood Dylan with his arms folded across his chest, staring down at Anna with an unknown expression in his eyes.

"Master?" she asked.

❋ ❋ ❋

Dylan didn't waste a single breath, giving Anna little time to prepare as he threw them both into the room behind him and stepped forward, kissing her on the lips. As their lips met, crashing roughly together, he groped her butt tightly.

Mmh!

The moan escaping her became swallowed by Dylan in another kiss. Somehow, he looked more desperate than usual. He lifted up her long dress and tried to wedge himself between her legs, startling her into pushing him away by the chest.

"*Haah...* If someone were to come by...!"

"I locked the door. Don't worry."

Anna gasped for air. Dylan enveloped her mouth in another kiss, one deep and passionate enough to make her lips swell. Soon enough, he got her to lie down on the bed, although it looked more like she had been pushed.

Unbuttoning his shirt and looking over her, he looked to be suffused with masculine vigor and virility, like a predator long since starved. It certainly wasn't easy for her to endure his lascivious gaze. He had yet to truly do anything to her, but she found her muscles tensing up in anticipation regardless.

His sharp eyes looked much more savage than

usual. Every time he freed himself from a layer of clothing, dropping the material onto the floor, she would gulp in concern.

"Why are you trembling so much?" he asked, tilting his head with genuine curiosity.

She stared at all the perfectly chiseled muscles he obtained through diligent exercise, her eyes roving over his toned abs before they landed upon his face at last. "Because I feel like you'll swallow me whole, Master," she answered.

Dylan grabbed her ankle and lifted it over the mattress. With both her legs propped up and spread apart by him, Anna was left gripping tightly onto the duvet.

"My thoughts go in the exact opposite direction, though. It had always been you hunting me down and devouring me this whole time, not the other way around, wasn't it?"

Following the vulgar claim that he uttered, he slid a hand underneath her skirt. His fingers caressed the thin white layer of silk that concealed her core, making her shiver. His fingers pressed down, dipping into her slightly whilst still obstructed by the fabric of her underwear, eliciting a faint moan from her lips.

Pushing her underwear to the side, his middle finger sought the source of the slick moisture escaping her, entering her with a twist. Her hips jerked up at the intrusion and he immediately pulled out his finger.

"Ah, no..." she protested weakly. Lifting her

head, she noticed he was using his dampened finger to measure how wet she had gotten.

He then lowered himself before her. She assumed he meant to move in and embrace her, but the thought was cut short as he pulled her underwear off her completely.

Her eyes widened as soon as she registered what he meant to do. "This is a bit too...!"

Dylan settled his face between her legs and soon she could feel his hot, soft tongue begin to lick into her, pushing through her bush. She writhed in place to cope with the foreign sensation, but she couldn't escape his firm grip upon her hips. He rolled his tongue carefully inside her like he would within a kiss. Anna could feel her resolve to flee fade from her.

Arousal coursed through her, traveling from her lower body to detonate and explode in an array of pleasure at the top of her head. Every time he swirled his tongue, thick, transparent liquid trickled out of her. She whimpered, moaning loudly.

"What is it?" Dylan asked her, lifting his head and licking his drenched lips. "Speak properly."

"More. Deeper," Anna begged, restless and aroused.

"Tell me that you want me."

"I want you, Master."

Yes. You want me as well. At last, a satisfied smile spread across his face.

He laid himself atop Anna and pushed his hard length deep within her. She tossed her head back so her chin sought the sky, her lips parted in an O.

"*Nnngh,*" Dylan groaned. As he slowly worked his hips, he quickly divested Anna of her clothes, her pale round breasts bouncing free like pudding. He leaned forward and bit into her earlobe. Then, he slid his lips down her neck before returning to claim her lips once more.

As he did so, Anna dug her fingernails deep into Dylan's back. All she could do was hold onto him as he pounded into her faster and more power-fully than he had ever before. He seemed to like how she clung to him.

She pulled at Dylan so he'd turn his neck to-ward her. Seeing the opportunity and refusing to let it pass, he kissed her once more and pushed his tongue into her mouth, entwining them so deeply neither could decipher which belonged to who.

She took her breasts in hand, but then her hands were pushed away by Dylan's own. It looked like he wanted control over everything. His jealousy was in full display, directly showcased before her. He gave her breasts a soft squeeze, then toyed with the hard-ened tips of their peaks with a finger, stimulating them. The whole room seemed filled with evidence of their heated exchange.

He thrust into her without giving her a moment to breathe, depriving her of the capacity to think properly. Every second felt like he was grinding her into dust. His fringe glistened with sweat. He had already come inside her once before, and now he was doing it again.

"*Haah.*"

Anna lay splayed out on the bed, devoid of strength. Dylan, meanwhile, still seemed to have some energy left. He immediately shifted his attention to biting into her breast. Although she knew she should speak up and confess that she could endure no more, seeing him selfishly embark on his desire to fondle and caress her was honestly a wonderful feeling.

Knock knock.

Someone was at the door. Her head snapped up in fear, but Dylan didn't pay it any mind.

"Someone's here!" Anna whispered, lowering her voice. She tried to get him to stop. It was only then that he let go of the nipple he had in his mouth.

"Don't worry about it," he said.

"How could I not worry about it?"

She pushed him aside and quickly stood up. A shadow descended upon his forehead. He spoke up, sounding annoyed. "See, no one answered so they left already."

Anna had already begun to dress herself, however, picking up her clothes and putting them on all at the speed of light. She dusted off her disheveled skirt. Dylan was lying in bed completely naked, so she gathered and organized his discarded clothing.

"Please dress quickly," she said. "Only then I can leave."

"Stay with me."

"Why are you acting like this again today? Did something happen?"

Her question reminded Dylan of his forgotten anger. His forehead wrinkled, cast in deep, displeased shadow. If one were to label his behavior as a ridiculous onslaught of jealousy, then so be it.

"From now on, don't hang out with my older brother," he spat. However, he regretted the thoughtless words as soon as they escaped him.

Anna felt as if her heart had frozen solid at that moment. "Why?" she asked. She slowly took her hand, which had been sitting on his shoulder, off of him. Her gaze bore straight into him. "Why are you forbidding me from being close to Master David?"

Dylan's lips were pressed tightly shut.

"Please tell me," she pleaded, and he finally opened his mouth.

"You really don't know?"

"Yes. I'm asking because I honestly don't know. I'm genuinely curious why you would say such a thing to me."

"No, you know very well. About that rumor."

Anna's face stiffened. "That rumor?" she echoed.

He chose not to explain any more than that. He knew she must've completely understood what he meant. Soon enough, she brought a hand to her head, her breathing turning rough.

"Yes, I know about that rumor very well. I've heard it with my own ears," she began. "But what about it? Why would that be any reason to stay away from him?"

A long silence followed her question, revealing

an answer as stiff in nature as the expression upon her face.

"You think... the rumor is true?" she breathed, disbelieving. Her eyes met his, now filled with resentment.

"If it's not true, then that just means you should be even more careful not to be seen beside my older brother. Even if your relationship with him is completely innocent, people will believe what they choose to believe. Should a little more time pass, that rumor will grow out of control!"

"Are you sure all of this isn't because only you, Master, choose to think this way?"

Dylan's eyes shook. "David acts as he does because he doesn't want to see you get hurt, either. Don't try to distort this."

Anna's eyes were wet, flush with tears ready to shed. She backed away from him. "If it's not the truth, why would I be hurt?" she asked. "It's not the truth, so why are you worried?"

"*Hah*, why would I be worried? I'm not worried at all."

"No, Master. You are. You're worried that the rumor is true! Was that why you were standing in front of the library and waiting like that? Because you doubted our relationship? You thought something might've happened in there!"

"Don't say 'our relationship'!" Dylan yelled vehemently. He felt as if her eyes were slicing and scratching away at his heart as she criticized him. "Don't describe your association with my older brother... like that."

"Master, you did not have the right to question me about the rumor as you did. Other people may whisper amongst themselves about it, but you, at least, Master..."

The tears welling up in Anna's eyes finally reached a breaking point, solemnly rolling down her cheeks.

"Shouldn't have to," she finished. Her expression was filled with resentment, disillusionment clear in her gaze. She glared at him, her eyes tinged red, before turning her back to him.

Dylan hurriedly reached for her, but she coldly slapped his hand away. Left behind in the chilling silence of the room, he watched the door close in front of him.

"Damn it!" he cursed, tossing his neatly folded clothes off his bed.

He felt like something was strangling his neck. The sensation wouldn't go away. Resting his hands upon his hips, he let out a deep sigh.

✳ ✳ ✳

Time kept passing. The atmosphere between Dylan and Anna remained cold, their relationship frozen. Circumstances didn't do much to help Dylan's cause; he couldn't find a single chance to properly apologize to her. He couldn't do anything besides allow time to pass meaninglessly by.

The more he ruminated on it, the clearer things

got. He was the one at fault.

He stuck a rock named Jealousy inside a snowball and kept lobbing it at Anna while pretending to care about her. He justified his actions by claiming that his worries were completely rational. In the end, it was just another means of arrogantly maintaining his suspicion of her. She wasn't someone who'd behave as the rumors claimed. More than anyone else, he should've believed in her.

Unfortunately, he didn't.

He couldn't even begin to come up with a means of apologizing to her. It was easy to wound her heart, but difficult to help mend it. Whenever their eyes would meet, her countenance would turn cold, and she'd pass him by without a care.

He honestly didn't know what to say to her, but he knew he couldn't let things remain as they were. Dylan began to fear that soon he would no longer be able to win her back.

"Anna," he called. Hearing him, Anna halted in surprise, stopping in the middle of the hallway. Although her name was the only one to leave his lips, Cathy, another maid she was walking with, stopped as well, staring up at him.

"So, like... there's a cricket in my room. Go in there and catch it," he said.

Cathy's face dissolved into an expression of utter fear at the mention of the cricket. She handed the job over to Anna. Anna looked annoyed at having to heed his command for the moment, but then she nodded her head and began the trek to his room alone.

Out of all things, why did he choose a cricket? He could've, at the very least, come up with a proper reason to bring her into his room. He felt like biting down on his tongue. Hard.

Cathy, having been left behind, spoke up in a friendly voice. "Is there anything you need me to do?" she asked.

"No."

Without sparing Cathy even a glance, he left to chase after Anna. Seeing him go like that, Cathy pouted, her feelings hurt.

❋ ❋ ❋

"Is it really true that there's a cricket in here?" Anna asked bluntly. Despite searching everywhere, she hadn't spotted even a shadow of a cricket in his room.

Dylan, who had been chasing behind her the whole time and trying to grab a chance to talk to her, nodded vigorously in assent, feigning innocence. "I definitely saw it with my own two eyes."

Anna looked skeptical. "Even so, as of right now, I don't see it anywhere. If it appears again in the future, you could call someone else to take care of it."

Cricket-less, she turned around to leave, but Dylan quickly caught her. "Y-you know how afraid I am of crickets. You must catch it now."

"But I can't find it."

"Search again. It may jump out somewhere."

Because of his stubbornness, she relented and began the search for the cricket of dubious existence once more. She really doubted it was there. Her expression didn't look very pleasant, but Dylan figured that it looked like that at the moment solely because she was in the same room as him.

He never could've predicted that she had an extreme fear of crickets as well. Anna assumed he gave her this task just to trick and frighten her.

Although he should never—as in, not in a million years—talk to her, he opened his mouth to speak.

"Hey, Anna—"

"*Eeek!*"

She screamed, cutting him off. She had lifted up the carpet without much thought, but at that instant, a brown cricket with long, thin legs and a pair of antennas jumped out from underneath it.

"No, wait. Why would there be..."

Falling into a paralyzed sitting position on the floor, Anna's eyes began to well up. Dylan, meanwhile, looked distraught. He didn't think it was possible for a cricket to actually appear.

The two panicked for different reasons. The cricket, the source of both their distress, looked satisfied with itself as if it had done its job by startling them. It jumped out the window.

Anna, legs trembling, barely managed to stand back up. "Now that the problem is solved," she said, "I'll be leaving now."

She left in a cold breeze. Since she disappeared so fast, he didn't even have the chance to stop her. Realizing that he didn't have the right to feel sad about her, he sighed deeply, blaming himself.

✳ ✳ ✳

"Get out," Carol ordered. She spoke with a voice as weak as her thinning face.

However, at that moment, David interjected with an opposing command. "No," he said. "You don't need to leave."

Anna stood in the middle between them, at a loss amidst their unexpected battle of pride. Husband and wife looked at each other as if they were gazing at their nemeses. Anna studied their expressions and carefully tried to raise her voice. This was not something she should be involved in

"Then, I'll—"

"I told you not to leave, didn't I?"

With a firm tone of voice, David essentially rooted Anna in place. All she came here to do was bring him some freshly brewed coffee at Madam Jane's behest, but then Carol arrived and all this began to unfold. Anna couldn't do anything but stand there awkwardly and take in the unfamiliar atmosphere.

"I have nothing to say to you, Carol, so please leave my study."

"You might not, but I do. That's why I need that child to leave. I want to talk about the problems in our relationship."

"Our relationship?" David's lips quirked into a smirk. Throughout their three years of marriage, a crack had formed and slowly began to grow between them, dividing them. "*Hah*," he scoffed. "I never thought I would hear anything like this come from your mouth. What was the catalyst that inspired your change of heart?"

His mocking tone made Carol stiffen and purse her lips. "I'll tell you everything. I'll tell you the whole truth. I'm just asking you to give me the chance," she said.

It was the first time Anna had ever seen Master David treat anyone with such harsh indelicacy, but it was also the first time she had ever seen Carol carry such determination in her voice. What was clear, at least, was that there was some kind of transformation taking place between them. Anna wouldn't even dare to think about interfering.

David continued, calm. "You're selfish to the end. I've tried for three years. For the last three years, I've continually requested conversations so we could solve the problem between us. Yet, what did you do?" He glared at her coldly, making Carol's eyelashes tremble. "You lied and deceived me."

He strode past her and violently swung open the door. Outside the study stood a wide-eyed nurse waiting for Carol, startled by the door's sudden movement.

"Leave," he commanded.

Carol's eyes were littered with teardrops. She bit down hard on her lower lip. With shivering hands, she took hold of her dress and slowly exited the room. However, either because her foot snagged on the door's threshold, or because she stepped on her dress, she immediately fell to the floor.

Oh no.

After seeing Carol trip, Anna readied herself to go and help her up, but at that moment, another person unexpectedly arrived and helped Carol instead.

It was Dylan.

"Carol!" he cried. He began to defend her, standing up to David. "Why are you doing this to her, Brother?"

"This isn't something you should involve yourself in," David replied.

As he spoke, Dylan spotted Anna still present within David's study and his expression grew hard. His gaze returned to his older brother, who wore a cold-hearted countenance.

"I know that. That's why I haven't done anything besides watch the situation unfold. I'm sure I'm not the only one this applies to; everyone else in the household is much the same," Dylan began. As long as Anna was inside that room, he couldn't keep turning a blind eye. "However, how much longer does our family have to keep tiptoeing around you two whenever you and Carol fight? Just for how long do our servants need to watch as you insult Carol right in front of them?!"

"You..!"

"Every single person in this household is keeping their eye on the both of you. Why don't you understand that you two are harming others with your never-ending psychological warfare?!" Dylan yelled.

David, becoming increasingly agitated, took a deep breath. "The person you're so worried about right now... do you consider her your sister-in-law..." His shivering hands were balled into a fist. Thin air escaped him as he spoke. "Or the woman you love?"

Anna felt all the blood drain from her body. Dylan, Carol, David, and Anna. None of them dared to open their mouths in reply.

Dylan froze like ice, while Carol kept her gaze directed to the ground, speechless. David's forehead creased with a frown, while Anna looked pale enough to faint.

✳ ✳ ✳

Anna sat hunched over with her arms wrapped around her body as she shivered. Earlier, following David's revelation, Dylan had grabbed her, and she frantically shook him off before running away. She hid where others' gazes would not reach, sitting at the corner of the stairs with betrayal and humiliation crawling deep within her.

"I feel like vomiting," she muttered between tightly pressed lips.

The reason he was so desperate to kick her out

of the household, why he claimed that the novel 'Yayok' was so similar to her, why he always seemed suspicious of her relationship with Master David, why he...

"If you ever hurt that person's feelings, I will pay back their pain tenfold. I'll make you experience more pain than their heart could ever feel by ripping yours out of your chest. Behave while you still have the chance."

She covered her mouth with her hand, stifling her sobs. All the sweet words he said and all the things he did for her were calculated. It felt like her world was crumbling apart.

"Anna!"

Dylan desperately called for her from afar. Anna cupped her ears with her hands.

"Anna!"

Unfortunately, a moment later a pair of black dress shoes came into view, stopping right in front of her. Anna immediately moved to get up and escape, but Dylan locked eyes with her and began to beg, taking hold of her.

"Please. Please let me talk to you for a moment," he pleaded, but he knew that it was already too late. He had already forsaken his chances to explain himself back when he kept despairing over trying to find the right words to say to her. An overwhelming sense of regret sat upon his shoulders.

"I no longer have anything to say to you, Master."

"I still have a lot of things I need to say to you,

though, so that's why—"

"Just what do you have to say? That nothing went as you expected it to? I ignored your warning, and as a result, my heart's been ripped to pieces just as you claimed it would be. Back then, I couldn't understand what you said to me, but now... I'm amazed at how clear things have become. I understand why you hated me so much this entire time."

"Anna..."

"Don't even try to give me excuses." She bit her lip, desperately holding back tears. "Three years ago, you lent me your hand and helped me through sorrow. As of today, however... You've pushed me into the deepest bowels of Hell."

Dylan couldn't respond. She continued, walking past him.

"Actually, it might've been better if I had never met you. The past few years where you've only appeared in my mind was much happier for me in comparison to your return back home."

He looked stunned, helplessly unable to take his eyes off her as she walked away from him. He wanted to catch her. He wanted to run before her and beg for her forgiveness, whining and crying, knelt upon the floor just to keep her with him. But, he couldn't. Dylan had to watch her walk away from him, too pitiful to reach out to her as she wobbled side-to-side. All the pain and despair she felt had been cursed upon her by his own influence.

Powerless, he couldn't do anything. At that moment, he was the most foolish man in the world.

✳ ✳ ✳

Everything was a mess. When did it all go wrong? Did it start when he began to misunderstand the relationship between Anna and his older brother, or did it begin when he genuinely started to fall in love with her?

No. In truth, it might have started when he came back home, just like she said. Tangled-up threads were of no significance once thrown away, so Dylan tried to act placidly by insisting to himself that it would all be okay if he just forgot her, but his efforts were futile.

He wanted to see her. The memories he made with her were precious and dear to him even if they were akin to a tangled mess of threads. He simply couldn't let them go.

Anna wasn't willing to work amongst the Kilner household anymore. Although she didn't say she was quitting, when she walked away from him, hatred in her eyes, Dylan knew it was all over. Nevertheless, he refused to give up on her because he couldn't bring himself to lose her. The more he admitted to himself that it was all his fault, the more certain he became that things couldn't end like this.

Late at night, Dylan brought a bottle of liquor to David's study. "It's me, Brother. It's Dylan," he called.

"Come in," David answered. He took his rimless glasses off and stood up from his chair.

He didn't ask what Dylan had come for. Instead, he wordlessly took the empty glass Dylan offered him and filled it with a drink. Then, they sat beside each other on a sofa atop the carpet.

"It seems like this is the first time I'm drinking alone with you," David mumbled, reminiscing with a distant tone of voice.

Dylan took a sip of his drink. The bitter taste burnt down his throat. "I left the house immediately after becoming an adult, that's why."

David shook his glass, looking to his companion as he drank. Dylan seemed like he had something to say, but David didn't hurry him, waiting quietly for him to open his mouth unprompted.

Instead of lighting a candle, the two brothers sat quietly, enjoying their drinks beneath the moonlight.

Clack.

Eventually, Dylan lowered his empty glass onto the table, making sure that it made a distinctive sound. After the long silence between them, the sound signaled that he was ready to converse.

"I have something I need to tell you, Brother."

David put his glass down as well, lifting his head. His eyes were firm, determination shining clear within their depths. He had prepared himself to hear these words a long time ago.

"It's about why I left home so suddenly three years ago," Dylan continued. David remained silent. "I dared to have feelings for your wife, Carol."

David didn't look astonished by the revelation

in the slightest. Dylan heaved a long, empty sigh. "Though, it looks like the both of you knew that already."

"Since we had a large age difference between us, you were a very unique brother to me," David began. "Our father spent most of his time working. I craved his love, and because of that, I wished that you, at least, would not live your life craving his love as I did.

"This is why I know how you feel. I had practically raised you since childhood, after all. I took care of you with my own two hands. The moment I brought Carol home to introduce her to everyone, your eyes kept gravitating toward her."

"That's right," Dylan said. "It was like that from the start. That's why I used going on a trip as an excuse to run away. When I returned three years later, however, I felt the firm resolve I had since developed fading from me completely. It turned out that I still had feelings for her, but..."

Dylan trailed off. David kept quiet, letting him continue.

"But now, after thinking about it, I realize that my feelings toward her were not of love, but of sympathy instead. I had endured for three years believing that if she, my sister-in-law, was happy with my brother, then that'd be fine. However, when I returned, I observed that she wasn't happy after all. Not even a little bit. I know I might be going out of line by saying this, but I resented you both."

"In the past, I, too, used to think that I could

make her happy even without love in my heart," David said. Then, he emptied the rest of the liquor left in his glass into his mouth. "However, Carol had a long-time lover. Someone other than me."

Dylan turned to David, surprised.

"I found out by chance while visiting Carol's parents' home," David explained. "They were talking about it. He was a chef that had worked for their family for a long time. Carol's household was poor and firmly opposed allowing her to remain with a servant working under her. They were forced apart and he had been fired.

"Carol lied to me about all of that and married me. She snuck behind my back and kept seeing him even after we were wed. Still, I couldn't be angry at her. One year ago, while I was heading back home, I saw him lying dead on the streets. That man."

Dylan couldn't stop his mouth from gaping open in shock. To think that this was the situation between David and Carol...

"Brother, I—" he began, but David shook his head.

"It's fine. What you said was all correct. It's been three years already. We can't keep pretending to be husband and wife like this. Not anymore."

Instead of looking depressed, David simply shrugged as if he felt refreshed now that the truth had been told. "Is that all you wished to say?" he asked. 'I'm sure you have more you want to mention,' his eyes seemed to say.

"There's also something else... I wanted to make

sure you know about this," Dylan said, lowering his head. "I no longer have feelings for Car—"

"So it's Anna now, isn't it?"

Dylan's head snapped up. A faint smile crossed David's face. "I told you. I figured it out because I know you."

Dylan didn't know what to say.

"I clearly remember when I first saw her. She entered the household three years ago, and when I asked how she came, she gave me a drawer key with your name engraved on it and suddenly asked me for a job."

Dylan's eyes clouded over for a moment, old memories finally returning to him. No... It was already too late. Why was it that he only remembered this now? Who Anna was, and how she got here.

To think that she was that young girl... At the time, she hadn't even grown out of her baby fat yet.

"Since it seemed like you had specifically requested it, I took care of her as best as I could. She was a brilliant and cheerful girl," David said. "During your three-year absence, I thought of the girl like you and treated her as such. The more I learned about her, the more I discovered how bright and intelligent she was. Even the silly little things she did from time to time looked cute. She also liked books, just like you did. Conversing with her brought new joy to my life. She was like the little sister I never had."

So that's how it was. *What brought them close together wasn't a book or some shared interest in one. It had been me,* Dylan thought.

Suddenly, he was overcome with the desire to see Anna again. It was greater than anything he had ever felt, and it had only been a few days since he last saw her.

Anguish descended upon Dylan's face.

"Dylan," his brother called. "Don't live like Carol and me. I do not wish for you to regret sending away the person you love, separated by the tall wall of reality. Nor do I wish for you to live your days exhausted and married to someone you don't even love. You know how horrible living like that would be, so I hope you don't repeat our mistakes."

"Brother..."

"I don't want to live such an unfortunate life, either. I felt as if I was barefoot and walking on thin ice these past three years."

The moment he said those words, David's eyes flashed with determination for a fraction of a second, almost as if he had made a monumental decision of some sort. Dylan couldn't figure out what David was planning to do, but he knew that he'd support whatever decision his older brother chose to make. Ultimately, it would pave the path toward a happy life for David and Carol.

* * *

"Why did you give up on the job, huh? Did you make some kind of mistake? Is that why?"

"You can't just say, 'Yes, I understand,' and

leave! Not even if they tell you to stop working! You have to get on your knees and beg for your life! It'll get colder from now on and we don't even have enough money for firewood to warm ourselves up, you know!"

"Honey!"

Without even bothering to listen to what her parents were saying, Anna went to bed right away, pulling the blanket to her head. She wished that everything was just a dream she could wake up from the next morning.

Just like her parents said, it would be harder to find a job later on, so she must find one before then. Reality, as cruel as it was, wasn't going to be easy on Anna, whose heart had been mercilessly beaten and bruised by the betrayal she suffered.

Soon enough, in a display of both fortune and, perhaps, misfortune, she was able to quickly find a new job thanks to Sebastian, her next-door neighbor. He recommended her as a babysitter for the household he worked in. She started working right away, trying her hardest to make sure thoughts of the Kilner household didn't leak into her mind subconsciously.

She was walking back home one day, exhausted after work, when someone suddenly called her name.

"Anna," came a familiar voice.

She stopped in her tracks. Behind a large tree, a dark shadow followed someone as they emerged from the shade. Anna's face was expressionless, but she bit the inside of her cheek. She didn't dare turn around. The place where she and Dylan had met for the first time was at that tree in particular.

Anna's fist, clasped right by her hip, tightened. Dylan called her name aloud once more, but she refused to respond. She started counting in her head.

One. Two. Three. Four.

As soon as she reached five, the number ringing loudly in her mind, she started walking again. She was still expressionless as if she couldn't see Dylan at all. As if his voice could not reach her.

✳ ✳ ✳

"Anna."

It happened the next day too.

"Anna?"

And the day after, as well.

Day after day was much the same. Dylan was always waiting for her beside the same tree on her path home from work. At this point, she was scared of the possibility that he might not be there when she reached the same place anymore. She'd grow relieved at the sight of his shadow beneath the tree cast by the moonlight shining behind him every time.

However, these feelings of anticipation and relief weren't welcomed in the slightest. Anna took hold of the cold, metal objects in her pocket and walked toward the tree.

"Let's have a discussion," she said. It had been

fifteen days since she had last properly talked to him, face-to-face. Fifteen days since she had left the Kilner family household.

Dylan watched her with pleading, puppy-dog eyes like a hound abandoned by the side of the street, nodding at her words. However, her face wasn't as bright and hopeful as his was.

"Please don't come here again."

Those were words she had been practicing saying to him dozens of times now. Hearing them, Dylan's face dropped, losing its smile. Regret and sorrow shrouded his expression.

It would've been normal to feel refreshed, to laugh at his face joyfully after seeing him in just as much pain as she had endured in the past. However, she wasn't happy. Not even a little bit.

Looking at his thin, pallid face only brought pain to her heart.

"It was all my fault," he uttered weakly. He spoke with a voice that sounded like it was drowning at sea.

"There's no use saying all that now," she said. "It's all over. I can't forgive you, Master. Seeing your face alone angers me to no end. How many of your words were the truth, and how many of them were lies? How many times have you laughed at me inside as you saw me easily play right into your hands? These thoughts have tortured me every day."

"I won't ask for forgiveness. I just wanted to say: I'll wait for you. I'll wait for the day you accept me one more."

"Don't even bother with waiting. I'm going to forget about it all, anyways."

Anna pulled the objects she held in her pocket out, presenting them to him. Dylan uncurled his once-frozen hands and brought them forward. She dropped the objects onto his palm.

They were the wristwatch and drawer key he had given her three years prior. He wordlessly looked down at the items in his hand.

"I don't want to see your face anymore, Master."

"I understand."

His sudden reply, devoid of hesitancy, left her speechless. She asked herself if she truly wished for him never to visit her anymore. Did she really want him to forget about her?

"I won't appear in front of you anymore. If that is your wish, I will do my best to grant it, but please at least allow me to stay behind you. I'll quietly remain where you won't see, so please at least allow me this much. Please don't take away my reason for living."

She sighed. "Why won't you understand? I'm going to forget everything. I'll erase every memory of you that I possess!"

"That's fine. Even if you do that—even if you never come back to me—I will never fault you."

Why was he behaving so foolishly? He had hated her and had lied to her this whole time, suspecting her of crimes she didn't commit, so why now?

"This is rather late, but can I ask one thing?"

She tilted her head curiously.

"Button, the one you mentioned was your friend, your family, and your sibling... did you find them?"

His voice sounded kind, just as he once did the day he first met her. It made Anna's heart feel weak. She lowered her head and shook it in denial.

"I see," he said. "That's all, then. It's cold, so you should go home."

He carefully tried to reach his hand out to pat her head, but she looked at him with caution in her eyes, making him pull back with a weak smile. She turned her back to him unhesitatingly. Again, the same as she had begun to do every day.

Once she disappeared from view, Dylan collapsed onto the ground, looking as if his life had lost all meaning. It wasn't like he didn't expect things to turn out like this, but it still hurt. Pain and anguish cut into him. Was this what it felt like to have one's heart ripped into pieces?

A single teardrop, illuminated by the moonlight, sparkled as it slowly fell from his eye.

SIx

"Waaah! Waaah!"

"Please don't cry, Master. I'll bring you some milk soon, so please just wait a little bit until then. Shh, shh."

With a two-year-old child on her back, Anna paced back and forth. She didn't rest even for a moment. The baby cried for almost every hour he was awake, earning him the title of 'Crybaby Young Master'. Comforting him, Anna released a tired sigh.

It wasn't simply that it was physically tiring work. Having to listen to the baby's crying all day long was torture she was forced to endure. After completing her work and walking home, her ears would be ringing. She'd hallucinate his screams in her sleep.

"Good work," Madam Shane said. "You can go back home now."

Her stomach was round and bulging since she was pregnant with another baby. At the sight of her, the child, amazingly, immediately stopped crying. He probably cried as he did to get his mother's attention above all else, Anna figured.

She bowed her head toward Madam Shane and adjusted her clothes before she began her walk back home. Every time she caught sight of the tree where Dylan would be watching her from afar, she would flinch slightly. She developed a habit of glancing toward it whenever she'd pass it even though she knew he'd no longer be there.

"Cold, isn't it?" Anna's mother greeted her. "Come in already. Have dinner."

She poured a serving of the cabbage soup boiling on the stove into a bowl and placed it before Anna at the table. While chewing on a piece of some hardened baguette, Anna's mother began to discuss a rumor she heard.

"It's about the Kilner family's youngest son. From the household you used to work at," she said.

Anna's hands stilled in the midst of ripping off another piece of bread.

"They say he's going to get married to a lady named Rin. I heard that a lot of witnesses saw them happily walking side-by-side. Sebastian's mother caught them walking out of a shoe shop together."

"From a shoe shop?"

"That's right. From what I've heard, the youngest son... yes, Master Dylan had given Lady Rin a red pair of shoes as a present from that shop. Since she received word from the shop owner directly, the rumors practically confirmed to be true," Anna's mother said. At that moment, without having even a single sip of her soup, Anna pushed her chair back and stood up.

"Oh my, why are you getting up so soon? Not hungry anymore?" her mother asked, confused. She suggested eating more, but Anna cited a loss of appetite and left for her bed right away.

"A full stomach helps you feel less cold," Anna's father said, siding with her mother. He was usually unfriendly, but now he tried to sound like he was concerned about her.

In response, Anna just snapped at him, saying, "I'm not hungry!" before leaving.

The couple, left behind, exchanged glances as if to ask, 'What's wrong with her?'. Since they were clueless, however, they just shrugged it off.

✳ ✳ ✳

Just as Anna had wished, Dylan stopped showing himself before her. Now, she regretted having said anything to him. Now that she could no longer see him, she couldn't determine whether or not he was still waiting for her or if he was off preparing his marriage to Lady Rin as the rumors claimed. She wasn't sure if he was breaking the promise he made to her wherein he said he would wait for her, or if he was off with that other woman.

Carrying the sleeping child she was tasked to look after, she looked out the window as the rain drizzled over the world beyond.

"Liar," she mumbled quietly. "Hypocrite."

She wanted to hate him. To resent and loathe him.

"Selfish to the end."

Fraught with the need to cut off her ever-growing longing for him and accepting of any method to do so, she bonked her head against the window. The sound woke the baby up, and its eyes flew open, crying loudly.

"Waaah!"

✳ ✳ ✳

"Would you like me to bring you the usual?" Betty asked.

The customer before her gave her a snow-white smile. "Please," he said. Although she knew it was simply a smile born of courtesy, she still blushed at the sight of it.

"The same today as well?" her boss asked her when she came to relay the order.

"Yes, he ordered the same stuff again. Beef stew and bread."

"How diligent of him. It's not easy to come in every day right when the shop opens." No matter how much of a regular a customer was, they still wouldn't visit every single day of the week. Yet, despite that fact, this handsome-looking man had started visiting the restaurant half a month ago without even a day's rest just to sit at the same place and order the same food. "It sorta feels like he has a story behind him, doesn't it?" Betty's boss mused.

Betty paused in the midst of setting up a table and nodded in acknowledgment. "Yes, I think he's got a romantic backstory spurring him on. You think he's waiting for someone he loves?"

"How are you so sure he's doing this for a romantic reason?" her boss grumbled. "It might just be that he had nothing else to do, so he found my shop by coincidence and fell in love with my cooking."

She stared at her boss in disbelief. "You're the one who mentioned him having a story behind him in the first place, you know?"

Betty left her boss after his sudden display of grumpiness and visited the customer in question, who sat blankly looking out the window beside him. Whether he was searching for someone outside or if he was simply deep in thought, she couldn't tell.

She placed a napkin, spoon, and fork in front of him before sparing a quick glance at his attractive face. He looked focused. In his eyes, she could feel longing, delight, and heartbreaking sadness altogether. Turning her gaze, she spotted the person who had captured her customer's rapt attention.

It was a young woman with black hair tied into a bun atop her head. She was walking by a shop whilst blowing into her small hands in an attempt to warm them. At the moment, it seemed like everything around the handsome young man seemed to cease, as if he was frozen in time. He was so captivated by the young woman that Betty couldn't even hear him breathe.

The young woman wore a beautiful face that didn't match her shabby attire. The customer couldn't take his eyes off of her, watching her until she disappeared from view. Unwilling to bother him, Betty carefully and quietly slipped away.

✻ ✻ ✻

It was a rainy day. Dylan was enjoying a strong cup of coffee in the restaurant he frequented after finishing his breakfast, reading a book. As he read, someone came by, pulled a chair up beside him, and sat down.

"Have you been well?" they asked.

When Dylan turned his head, Rin was sitting by him, and, a moment later, an order of strong coffee — just like Dylan's—arrived in front of her. Other patrons of the restaurant glanced at the two periodically, recognizing them. They began to converse in a friendly manner.

"So, we meet again," he said. He had met her here a few days ago by coincidence.

"Yes. Well, I do keep finding you in this particular seat whenever I come here, after all," she said.

It would've been stranger if I didn't encounter you, though, since I specifically visited this restaurant with the intention of seeing you again. I knew that you'd be here every day, she thought to herself.

Dylan smiled back at Rin as if he could read her mind. Although the rest of the men in the village craved her attention, seeking to obtain even the slightest ounce of it, Dylan differed, caring so little about her that it actually seemed a bit mean. While she would ask all sorts of things—like if he had eaten, or what kind of book he was reading, or when he was planning to return home—all he did was politely answer her, never asking any questions of his own.

As Rin took a moment to come up with a question she could ask today, the restaurant's doors opened, bringing forth the sound of a ringing bell. Cold wind twirled to caress her thin, exposed neck, and she shivered lightly.

"Cold today, isn't it?" she asked, holding her cup of coffee with both hands as she looked to Dylan. In response, he just nodded, offering her an awkward smile. She didn't notice how his eyes were shaking.

His gaze was focused on Anna, who had just entered the establishment to buy some freshly baked bread. Extremely embarrassed upon noticing his presence, she only wanted to give him a quick glance, but then their eyes met.

Sipping on her coffee, Rin suddenly came up with something to talk about. She lifted the hem of her dress to reveal to Dylan the red shoes she wore. "Oh, yes, I wore these shoes today. The ones you bought for me, Young Master."

"I-Is that so. They fit you as well as I thought they would," Dylan replied, looking toward Anna and trying to keep his eyes on her even as he stammered.

"Have you given that one pair you bought to that child you mentioned hurt their foot?" she continued. "I wonder if they know the truth of it. You paid several times more than the original price of those shoes just to find the right size."

Instead of answering, his gaze lowered to Anna's feet. The shoes she wore, visible beneath the dampened hem of her dress, were not the ones he bought for her. *What were you expecting?* Dylan thought to himself as he smiled bitterly. He returned his attention back out the window. He should've been thankful that he had been given the opportunity to breathe the same air and occupy the same space she was.

Anna, meanwhile, was just as flustered by the situation. Since Madam Shane's mother had arrived, the baby had been put in her care for a moment, freeing Anna up for a different errand involving buying some bread. However, she ended up finding him here of all places. And, that wasn't all of it, either. Lady Rin was sitting right next to him.

So the rumor was true, she thought. It felt as if her

heart had stopped. There was a massive difference between hearing about something and witnessing it with your own two eyes. The amount of hatred she felt for the beautiful Lady Rin right then, as Dylan directed his smile toward her, made Anna furious to no end. She wished his life would always be terrible, realizing that she would always regret not cursing at him and smacking him as much as she could back when he was begging for her forgiveness.

"You bought those shoes on that day, right?" Rin asked.

"That day? What do you mean?"

"I mean, that time you saved that girl on the streets. People praised you endlessly for your actions on that day. It's reached the point where there isn't anyone in town who doesn't know about your heroic deed."

Anna took a deep breath. It still hurt to think about that moment. Seeing Dylan struck down and hearing the harsh sound of a slap as the drunken man's hand met Dylan's face terrified her. Back then, she had been scared he'd never wake up again.

"That's right," Dylan said. "I bought them on that same day, didn't I?"

"I heard that you got a huge bruise because of it, so I tried to bring some ointment to you. I tried to deliver it to you myself, but it seemed like you weren't home at the time because Madam Jane informed me that you hadn't been in your room. I was left with no choice but to leave the ointment to Madam Jane so she could deliver it to you."

Dylan glanced over at Anna again. He hadn't known that Rin had been the one to provide the ointment that Anna helped him apply.

"Did you put it on?" Rin asked.

"...Yes."

These hands of mine had put the ointment directly on his face, Anna thought, as she looked down at her palms. Even then, however, he had been more worried about her injured foot than his own face. She knew the truth. He intentionally bought those shoes for her, and he fabricated an excuse just in case she got too insecure to accept his generosity otherwise.

When she broke that plant pot, he had treated her harshly, but as soon as he realized she had cut her foot on the broken shards, he personally treated her wounds. With a conscientious expression upon his face, he made sure not to touch her wounds so that they would hurt less.

She wanted to believe that his careful treatment of her at the time wasn't one of the lies he had constructed for her.

"In any case, it looks like the rain is getting heavier."

"You're right."

The memory of the day Dylan and Anna spent in the hut, stranded by the heavy rain, returned to her. Then came the memory of when he saved her from danger at the party. Then, the memory of him standing by her side when Samantha yelled at her.

All the memories she had turned her back on and tried to ignore this whole time began to rise to the forefront of her mind. She had covered them up by disguising them as nightmares, but now that she was made to confront them once more, she realized that none of them felt like nightmares at all. She didn't want to let go, lose, or allow those happy memories to be forgotten with time, either. At all.

"Tomorrow, Ena... I mean, there'll be a party at Mr. Chess's. Will you come?"

"No," Dylan said, "I'm afraid I won't be able to go."

"Do you have a prior engagement planned? It would be great if we could go together."

"Not because of any plans... I just need time to reflect deeply upon my mistakes and mend my ways."

Rin tilted her head curiously. "May I ask what mistake you've made?"

Right then, Betty emerged from the kitchen. "I'm sorry," she said. "The bread hasn't finished baking yet, could you wait a little long—huh?" She looked in Anna's direction. Her eyes immediately widened in surprise.

It was that young woman. The one that the handsome customer came in every day to catch a glimpse of.

"I will wait," Anna answered quietly, nodding.

Still by his seat conversing with Rin, Dylan's next few statements, escaping him as if they were choked by tears, entered Anna's ears with staggering clarity.

"I had inflicted unto someone an injury which I

cannot wash clean," he said. "I had carelessly misunderstood them and harassed them. I didn't give them the same amount of trust they had given me in their earnest reliance. I stole their happiness and had forgotten them. But, my biggest regret was..."

Anna's eyes welled up with tears.

"...That I wasn't able to tell her that I loved her—that I truly loved her—even once."

Rin's expression was a confused mixture of things as she looked at him. "Ah..."

"I loved her with all my heart," Dylan said. He looked deep in thought. Then, he stood up. It seemed like he was going to leave earlier than Rin for today. "Thank you for hearing me out," he said. "I'll pay for your coffee as thanks."

He gave Betty a meaningful glance and she immediately caught his intentions, nodding in assent. The restaurant door's bell rang and a wave of cold air rushed through the room, signaling his exit. At that, Anna finally turned, properly watching as his figure grew farther away beyond the window.

The restaurant's chef looked at Dylan's empty seat and raised his voice, speaking as if he had just witnessed a rarity. "What's with him, leaving so early today? He used to sit there from the moment we open to the moment we close."

Perhaps he had been waiting for her every day, Anna realized. Was he running away like that so he could obey her wish and stop himself from appearing before her again? At that thought, Anna gasped thinly.

"The bread's here," the chef said to Betty. "Get it wrapped up for her, quickly."

Betty poked at the chef's pudgy hips a few times, lifting her index finger to her lips to encourage him to leave Anna be. Anna was obviously contemplating an important decision, and Betty genuinely wanted her to be braver.

It seemed like an eternity passed in that brief moment that occurred before Anna made her mind and hurriedly turned to leave the restaurant. The chef, oblivious to the situation at hand, yelled out to her as she left.

"What about your bread?!" he shouted.

Betty just looked at him and shook her head.

✳ ✳ ✳

Anna threw herself outside into the rain. It was getting heavier. She looked around, trying to find Dylan. Passersby looked at her like she was insane, but there was no time to care about how others thought of her. His handsome face, his voice—which only sounded friendly when directed toward her—and the scent of his warm body, enticing enough to make her never want to leave his embrace... she longed for it all. Everything about him drove her wild.

Finally catching up with him, she began to yell.

"Why would you hide just because I told you not to come anymore?!" she screamed. "You should have kept coming even if I told you to disappear!

You should've come even if I said I never wanted to see you ever again!"

He recognized her voice and turned around. "Anna?" he asked, surprised. She chased him down in the pouring rain, and, having forgotten her umbrella back at the restaurant, she bore the cold with just the clothes on her back.

He hurriedly ran up to her. She continued to speak.

"How was I to know if you were still behind me? If I can't see you, how am I supposed to know if you were really waiting for me, or if you left because you had a change of heart?!"

She burst into tears like a child. Although she knew her complaints didn't make any sense, she still wanted to say them to him, because the truth was that she didn't want to lose him at all. She hated and resented him, but she behaved as she did because she loved him just as much.

This was what she wanted to say to him.

Suddenly, she realized there wasn't any rain falling on her head. Dylan had tilted his umbrella over her, leaving him to get soaked from head to toe. He looked down upon her with lowered eyes.

Seeing his thinning face, her heart crumbled into pieces. He must have thought himself a sinner, constantly whipping himself for the crimes he had committed. Her heart ached at the sight of him. An overwhelming sadness suffused her sense of being.

"I love you," she told him.

She never wanted to see him weak and devoid

of energy, or overcome with sadness and writhing in pain ever again, and that was because she loved him.

It was just that simple. As a person, she respected him, liked him, and, more than anything else, loved him dearly.

"...What did you just say?" he asked, disbelieving.

"I said that I love you. I really love you. To be honest, I wanted to find another man and show off how happy I was living without you. I wanted to return to you only after my hair had turned gray and my heart started turning around." Although it was a fruitless effort, she wiped away some of the tears spilling out of her eyes. "That's what I was planning, but seeing you suffering because of me made my chest hurt. You're the one who talked about waiting for me, but I'm the one who's worrying the most! This is way too unfair!"

The moment Anna finished speaking, Dylan grabbed her cheeks and kissed her lips. His umbrella fell to his feet and the two shared a deep, heartwarming kiss that stunned everyone watching.

People began crowding around them.

"I love you," Dylan said, his voice quivering as he barely held himself together. "I love you; I love you."

The words he always regretted not saying to her continually poured from his mouth, finally achieving his long-standing desire. They smiled at each other, then he kissed her deeply once more. Then, he took hold of her hand and ran through the crowd that had gathered around them, sprinting together through the rain.

The young couple looked as if they didn't care at all that people had been staring at them. The on-lookers around them began to dissipate once they left. The long black umbrella Dylan dropped rolled across the ground.

Around five—no, six steps away from where the reunited couple once stood, two other umbrellas were rolling on the ground similarly to Dylan's own forgotten one. However, they were dropped for an-other reason entirely.

"Those two people just then..." Samantha trailed off, at a loss for words.

"They were Master Dylan... and Anna," Cathe-rine, another maid, finished for her.

The two of them stood there for a long time, completely stunned as if they had been hit clubbed on the head.

✹ ✹ ✹

If this was all a dream, then the sun would not rise the next morning. Dylan, naked from head to toe, brushed Anna's hair behind her ear as she laid beside him. They had already climaxed together whilst holding hands a moment prior, and now they rested, covered in sweat and panting heavily.

Dylan leaned over and kissed her on her forehead and her cheeks. "It feels like I'm still dreaming," he whispered. Anna looked up at him with her gaze half-lidded, taking in his roughened breathing. His arousal hadn't completely subsided yet.

"Me too," she answered.

Dylan stroked her spotless back, his hand traveling downwards to stroke her sleek hips and her plump bottom. He pulled her left leg up over his hip, sliding his hardened member against the valley between her thighs. It shone as it stood in stark relief, moistened with pale fluids dripping down its length.

He licked her lower lip enticingly. "Should we do it once more?"

Anna wrinkled her nose and smacked his chest half-heartedly. "Asking that way is cheating—*ah! Mnh!*"

Grinning playfully, he grabbed his rod and guided it between her sensitive, pink flesh until he found her entrance. In one swift thrust, he pushed himself inside of her.

Haah… haah.

They touched foreheads, halting for a moment so they could simply feel each other's warmth and breathe.

"Look at me."

Heeding Dylan's request, Anna lifted her head, and as soon as their eyes met, he gave her a quick kiss on the lips before slowly rotating his hips. He began to move within her, seemingly filling her up without leaving any room to spare. Performing the most elegant maneuver in the world, he shifted his hips slowly, forcing her to feel every inch of his thick, throbbing length as it gradually pierced her.

At first, she moaned, satisfied with the sensation, but as time passed and he kept his speed consistent, she began to feel restless. Anna began to beg for a change, her voice heartbroken.

"A... a little bit more," she pleaded.

"*Haah...* what?"

"Like, just a little bit more..."

She was so wound up that instead of elaborating, she pushed him down further into the bed and climbed on top of him. She proved that actions spoke louder than words as she propped herself up with her hands braced upon his chest, gyrating her hips with his manhood now lodged deeper within her.

Breathy moans, akin to thin whispers, escaped from his lips. Anna leaned forward and lifted herself up a little. Half of his length, covered in their combined juices, briefly slid free from her before it disappeared inside her once more as she sank back down. She moved her hips rapidly from the start. As opposed to Dylan's slow, yet graceful methods, her technique was more passionate and aggressive.

She straightened her back. Every time she bounced herself up and down upon him, her round breasts would lewdly bounce with her. He stretched his hand out and took one of her soft, pliant breasts to sit beneath his palm. Then, he twisted one of her hardened nipples, coaxing a low growl from her as her muscles tightened around his shaft.

He gasped at the sensation. She had already felt tight, but every time he kneaded her breast and pinched their taut peaks she'd clench down on him even harder. It took his breath away. He laid there for a moment simply at her mercy, enjoying the ecstasy she brought him before he finally began to move with her. Whenever Anna would lower herself onto him, he would meet her descent by slamming his hips up into her. She would scream out a moan that sounded as if it were a mixture of both crying and laughter. Soon enough, a hot, indescribable feeling began to settle between her legs.

Primal instinct told her that he was about to explode within her. If she were together with him, she would willingly endure their impending climax even if it meant their deaths.

Their faces were flushed a heated red. They reached the precipice of their arousal at the same time.

"Oh, Anna!"

Before, it had always been Anna that came first, but this time things were different. Dylan came hard, passionately crying out Anna's name as the fruit of their love spread deep within her. At that moment, she reached the height of her pleasure and fell against his chest, trembling, as if she were a handful of ash.

✹ ✹ ✹

"Come in."

Madam Jane stepped into Dylan's room. He was preparing to leave the house, fixing his clothes using his reflection in the window to ensure that nothing was wrong.

He turned to Madam Jane with suspicion in his eyes. She had entered in silence, uttering not a single word. "Did you have something you wanted to say to me?" he asked her.

"Are you going somewhere?" she asked in return. When she spoke, genuine worry dripped from every syllable, but then she kept going as if she hadn't actually intended to wait for Dylan's answer. "Your father needs to tell you something."

She then left the room first, a shadow descending upon her face. Dylan maintained an unexpectedly calm and expressionless demeanor as he followed her down the stairs.

When he arrived at the reception room, Sir Crane and David were sitting on a sofa waiting for him to arrive. Even Carol was there.

"Did you call for me, Father?"

Amongst the room's heavy atmosphere, Dylan looked to be the only one who remained undaunted and relaxed.

Sir Crane surveyed Dylan's clothing as his son took a seat upon the sofa. "It seems like you're planning on going somewhere," he said, a deep shadow crossing his forehead.

"It seems to me that Father and Mother both have the same inquiry."

They looked at him questioningly.

"And you both know where I plan to go and who I'm going to see." Dylan pulled up his sleeve, glancing at his wristwatch. "So, I'll have to ask for this to be a short discussion, please. I could end up late to my appointment."

Sir Crane coughed a loud, audible 'ahem!' as if he disapproved of Dylan's behavior. "It looks like you're going out to meet that girl," he said. "The one that worked in our household before she stopped coming."

"Yes. Her name is Anna Maius."

"I heard that she's working as a nanny in another household now. I hope that there isn't another young man like you living there, otherwise, I'd be worried."

David, sitting next to Sir Crane, interjected. "Father!" he called, attempting to discourage the older man from continuing.

Dylan realized that his father intended to anger him with words. And, it actually worked. He got mad. It didn't matter to him if Sir Crane called him stupid or an idiot, but he refused to permit anyone making fun of Anna in such a way, even if the person in question was his very own father.

His hand balled into a tightly clenched fist. "You know, Father," he began calmly, "I do not wish to live like you."

"What?"

"Our family always came second to you. You spent your entire life prioritizing money, fame, and your reputation. That's why, ever since I was young, I've always considered you an outsider in my heart. Not once have you regarded me in a friendly manner, forgoing even just turning to me and asking, 'Have you had dinner?'. And, to top it all off, you still manage to confuse my age sometimes."

Sir Crane remained silent, momentarily unable to respond.

"In a way," Dylan continued, "I think I'm glad. You helped me realize that, with you around, I can't possibly end up the worst husband or father in the world."

"Dylan!" Madam Jane cried, pale and shocked.

He turned to face her. "I will live my life seeking happiness rather than chasing after money and fame. Is that so wrong?"

"How do you expect yourself to survive doing as you please and looking only at what you want to see?! Butterflies in your stomach and your heart pounding? Those feelings are only temporary!" Madam Jane exclaimed. "The mistake of mixing the noble blood of our Kilner family together with the blood of that poor household devoid of history, on the other hand, will last an eternity. What do you think others will think of us? They will forever look down upon our name. If you think about how people will be gossiping behind our backs, talking about how dirty blood has stained our family..." She looked so agitated that the veins on her forehead were bulging. "Doesn't that sound horrifying to you? Everyone's gazes focused on you?"

Dylan squeezed his eyes shut and shook his head. "I think that you're making it more horrifying than it is, Mother. The moment Father began to amass his fortune was the moment our reputation began to soar and our blood became clean."

"Why are you acting like this Dylan?! What is that girl to you?"

"If disgracing our name is the only thing you're worried about, Mother, then there's only one solution," he said, rising from his seat as if he had made a decisive choice. Everyone's gazes fell onto him. "If you oppose mixing Kilner blood with commoner blood, then I'll cast aside that identity. Neither Anna's family name nor her poverty will be enough to justify splitting us apart. I'm not committing a sin by doing this. The fact that you're judging others by this basis is the real sin."

"Y-you...! Are you threatening your own mother right now?!"

"No. Instead, I'm begging you. Extremely earnestly. Please acknowledge Anna and judge her solely for who she is. Help me achieve happiness."

Dylan, concluding his speech, looked back and forth between his shell-shocked parents. Then, using long strides, he quietly left the room.

Madam Jane placed her hand upon her head, sighing as she flopped back onto the sofa. "What should we do now?" she asked.

"He'll give up sooner or later," Sir Crane scoffed. "Just assume that he's bluffing."

Carol, who, up until now, had been sitting quietly during the conversation, finally spoke up. "I wish for Dylan's happiness."

"What?"

"I was amazed by his confidence and bravery. I'm sure it wasn't easy to confront us like that," she said, a faint sadness crossing her eyes.

"Mother, Father," David said, joining in, "please be satisfied with just me living in accordance with your will."

"David, even you?!"

"You know how my wife and I have spent our days after adhering to your expectations. Do you still want to stop Dylan?"

Madam Jane's face contorted. She knew what they had become. That was why she was always worried about Carol and why she tried her best to persuade David. She thought that if she could manage something between them, they wouldn't need to walk the path of loneliness and pain she had endured her whole life.

The relationship between her and her husband was a negligent one. He was almost always away from the house. At one point, because of the overwhelming sorrow consuming her, she had to contain the impulse to jump out of an empty window whilst breastfeeding David, who had only recently been born at the time.

She started getting a headache. Even though enough time had passed to forget it all, the memories were still a deep wound residing vividly in her mind.

"Father and Mother," David called.

Sir Crane and Madam Jane were in deep thought for different reasons. However, the sight of David and Carol looking at them, determination writ plain on their faces, blew a cold wind through Madam Jane's heart.

"We have something we need to tell you as well."

* * *

"Then, Master David and Lady Carol have...?" Anna trailed off.

"They aren't going to divorce," Dylan said, "but they did say that they won't be having a child."

"Ah..."

Anna felt sorry for David and Carol. 'Perhaps marrying without love is like making potato soup without any potatoes,' she thought as she lifted a spoonful of potato soup into her mouth.

"I'm sure it must've been a huge shock for the madam. One of her children said they'd give up their family name while the other said they'll never have a child."

"What can you do, anyway? If she couldn't handle that, she would've given up on everything long ago."

"Even so, she's your mother. Aren't you being too cold about this?"

"I'm not the cold one here, our mother is. Other

mothers would consider the happiness of their children their first priority, right?"

"You're right, but..."

"I'm confident that I'll be a father who puts his children first."

Cough! Cough!

Hearing Dylan's overconfident declaration, Anna began to cough, quickly turning the dining table before her into a mess. He asked why she couldn't believe him while she, her four-year-old younger sibling, her father, and her mother all began to choke on their soup, coughing until their faces grew flushed.

"When are you planning to go back to your house?" Anna asked, recovering.

Dylan's expression turned sad. "You want me to go back?"

"No, that's not it. But..."

After Dylan started living with them, her parents began to talk much less frequently. Just seeing how the variety of dishes being served during meals had increased made her realize how much her mother cared for Dylan even though she didn't outright say so.

"Oh, yes. Anna, about your sibling, Button."

"Button?"

"No matter how much I tried, I couldn't find Button. I couldn't find any mention of the name in this town or the next," Dylan said.

"Well, that's a given. How could we hope to

find Button now? It's already been three years. Button may still be Button to us, but their new owner could've changed their name."

As Anna spoke about her lost family member, guilt seemed to cloud her father's face. Her tone, however, sounded relatively calm and neutral, confusing Dylan. Then, her father spoke up.

He coughed awkwardly. "It's all my fault in the end," he confessed. "I condemn myself for drinking so much. Back when I was desperately thirsting for a drink, I spotted that dog tied to the tree and —"

Dylan doubted his own hearing. "Did you... did you say 'dog'?"

"Yes, Button is a dog," Anna answered. "Didn't I tell you that Button was a baby dog I picked up from the streets?"

It wasn't anyone's fault. In the end, it was just a small case of miscommunication. Nevertheless, Dylan couldn't help but feel a bit annoyed. To him, it felt like Anna had him fooled big time.

✳ ✳ ✳

Dylan didn't care about the gazes following him. He held Anna's hand securely as they walked through the crowded town. It had been one week since he had left the Kilner family household.

"Do you know where we are now?" he asked Anna.

"Of course," she answered confidently.

Here, town buildings were spaced farther apart,

leaving more space between them. Trees appeared in greater numbers, their once beautiful green coats now shed, leaving their branches bare to the wind. After walking diligently for a while through the forest they encountered, a field of pristine white snow came into view. It looked as if no one had passed through the area yet.

The sparkling lake that was once there lay concealed beneath the snow and ice that blanketed its surface. Although its beauty could no longer be seen, the area was still a magnificent sight to behold.

"Wait," Dylan said, stopping them for a moment. He had noticed Anna's cheeks were red and plump because of the winter breeze's cold sting, so he pulled off the scarf he was wearing around his neck and wrapped it around hers instead.

"I can't breathe," Anna gasped, her eyelashes fluttering as she pawed at the scarf covering her face. She wiggled, timidly protesting Dylan's overprotective behavior.

He pointed to the transparent cloud that escaped the folds of the scarf. "It looks like you're breathing well enough to me. It's better than getting a cold."

Then, he locked their fingers together again, resuming their walk.

She went along with him for a moment. However, after a few steps, she looked up at him as she squinted her eyes in suspicion and asked, "Why have you been acting like this lately?"

"What do you mean?"

"Recently, you've been way too overprotective of me."

"You're worried even though I'm being nice to you?"

"I'm worried because you're being nice to me."

Dylan smirked. Not only was it cute that she never backed down from anything he said, but it was also amusing how he didn't notice until now how simple her thoughts were.

"I have confidence that I'll be able to treat you even better from now on."

"Huh? Why are you saying that all of a sudden?"

Dylan suddenly grabbed Anna's arm, stopping her. His beautiful, clear face seemed to shine brightly, the light reflecting off of the snow accentuating his features. However, his dignified, dark eyes were more serious than they had ever been before.

He took her by the shoulder and turned her in the direction of the forest.

"I knew it," she exclaimed. "This was where the hut wa—"

Suddenly, Anna was at a loss for words. She was so surprised she forgot to breathe for a moment.

Although she was looking right at it with her own two eyes, she still couldn't believe it. Where there definitely should've been a run-down hut, ready to fall apart at any moment, there was something else instead. The hut was gone, and in its place stood a tidy, yet sturdy-looking cottage sitting atop the snow.

It was like magic.

Am I allowed to be this happy? she thought. She raised her hands over her mouth in astonishment.

"Huh?"

But Dylan's surprise gift didn't just end there. One of the fingers covering her mouth was sparkling in the light. A ring inset with a blood-red jewel lay wrapped around her ring finger. She hadn't noticed until now.

After a while passed wherein she remained silent, simply staring at the ring on her finger, Dylan became hesitant. "Why aren't you saying anything?" he asked.

"I received so many things in such a short amount of time... I didn't expect them at all... I can't keep my head on straight," she finally answered.

Hearing her whine about being too happy made him laugh aloud. This miracle she was experiencing must've felt like finding the ocean in the middle of a desert.

Slowly, she walked toward the house which would soon serve as their future haven. The closer she came toward their new home, the clearer the cottage shone in her eyes.

"It was after we returned from our stay at the hut. Upon that day, I began to sketch this house in my mind, constructing my image of it right away. The beautiful forest, the lake, and you standing in the middle of it all. You were someone who shined so brightly that the word beautiful would never be enough to perfectly describe you. This whole house was built just for you. Only you."

Anna put her hands on Dylan's winter-chilled cheeks.

"Should you permit it," he continued, "then, from now on, I'll do better than ever before. I will treasure and love you more than anything else."

She looked into his eyes and couldn't find a single lie, realizing once again what a wonderful, heart-pounding blessing it was to love someone who truly loved her back. Rising onto her tiptoes, she brought a kiss to his lips. "Before I met you, I was insignificant," she told him. "Now, I feel as if I've become someone a bit more special."

"You are special. That's why I've given you all of my heart."

"Thank you. And I love you. I'm sorry that all I can offer you in return is my love."

"That love is enough."

Dylan kissed her on the forehead. Then, he paused. "Well, to be honest, there is one more thing I want from you..."

"What's that?"

His eyes, which had been gazing into her own, seemed to change slightly. "It's cold, so let's talk about this inside."

"At least tell me what it is," Anna insisted. "If it's something I can give you, I'll go wherever I need to in order to bring it to you."

Did she not know what he wanted? Anna was fired up and confident, not realizing the wicked thoughts Dylan was cooking up in his mind. As opposed to clarifying, he simply kissed her on the forehead once more, a confident smile of his own dawning on his face as he opened the house's front door with a click.

❋ ❋ ❋

Three months later.

Even though an hour had passed, Anna still hadn't left her spot in front of the mirror. She wore a thin violet dress handpicked for her by Dylan, and her black hair bounced atop the cleavage on her chest.

"Do you think tying it up would be better?" she asked.

Hearing her voice, Dylan's head snapped up from the newspaper he was reading. It seemed like he was waiting for her to finally ask him that question directly.

"I was on the side of leaving it down in the first place," he answered. "Actually, you know, about that dress—the neckline didn't seem that revealing when I first bought it. Perhaps the seller made a mistake and sent you a different one."

"Yep," Anna said, completely ignoring Dylan's opinion, "I definitely think tying it up would make it look cleaner." She deftly tied her hair above her head and fixed it in place with a pin. "How do I look? There's nothing weird, right?"

Dylan put down his newspaper and walked up

behind her as she was carefully studying every ounce of herself in the full-length mirror.

"I'll always be beside you, so there's no need to be nervous." He hugged her from behind, leaving a kiss mark on her slim, uncovered shoulder.

"Thanks," she laughed, turning around to hug him tightly in return for reassuring her.

Today was the day she was set to visit Sir Crane and Madam Jane. She was to appear not as a maid, but as Dylan's partner. Her insides felt queasy; she was nervous enough that she was trembling slightly. Dylan calmly stroked her back with his warm hands as he held her, trying to ease away some of her anxiety.

✵ ✵ ✵

The carriage drove across the Kilner family's wide, open yard. Watching the mansion come closer and closer through the carriage's window, Anna was deep in thought, reminiscing on the memories the mansion brought her.

In the past, she had stood inside Dylan's room on the third floor, looking down to watch him exit his carriage from afar. Now, she was sitting next to him inside of it as they waited to arrive together. Back then, she never could've imagined herself looking at him with warmth in her eyes, talking about the love they had for each other.

"What are you thinking about so deeply?" he asked. She smiled and shook her head.

"Nothing at all."

It didn't seem like it was nothing, so he was about to ask her more about it, but before he could, the carriage finally stopped in front of the mansion.

She started feeling queasy again. Unconsciously, she took hold of Dylan's hand and squeezed it tight.

"I know you're feeling uncomfortable about this meeting," he began, "but please try to believe it'll be a pleasant experience. It's fine to make mistakes, and it's natural to feel a little awkward. So... what I mean to say is: you don't need to try to look perfect."

He looked deep into her eyes, nodding firmly as if to give her strength, so Anna nodded back in response. Then, the carriage door opened, and, along with it, the mansion front door.

Sir Crane, Madam Jane, Master David, and Lady Carol all walked out one by one. Inside the mansion were numerous other relatives peeking out of the windows to catch a glimpse at Anna's face.

"Let's get off," Dylan said, offering Anna his hand to help her off the carriage. They alighted from the carriage and neared the mansion

"Welcome," Sir Crane greeted awkwardly. Anna curtseyed. Madame Jane, meanwhile, didn't look very well, still not over the fact that Dylan had left the house.

Dylan smiled and kissed the back of her hand. "Thank you for giving us permission, Mother."

She looked grumpy when she finally opened

her mouth to speak. "The whole town is rife with rumors already, so there's no use in staying stubborn, anyways," she sighed.

Dylan exposed his white teeth in a pleasant smile.

"It's cold outside," David interjected, pointing to the front door, "so why don't we finish our greetings inside?"

Dylan placed his hands on Anna's shoulders as they both ascended the stairs. As she passed by, Anna saw Samantha and Casey standing to the side, their gazes lowered to the ground.

Later on, Anna, momentarily left standing alone, was approached by David and Carol, the latter of which handed her some champagne.

"You and Dylan look much better than you did before," David said. Then, he caught himself. "Ah, goodness me. I shouldn't talk to you with such familiarity. I think it will take some time for me to get used to referring to you as a formal member of our family."

Hearing that he was recognizing her as an actual part of the family brought goosebumps to Anna's arms. "You can continue to treat me as you did in the past. That's more comfortable for me."

"We can't do that. We have to set an example so that the rest of the household respects you as well," Carol said.

David nodded in agreement. "That's right."

It looked like David and Carol were much closer and more intimate than they were before, making Anna's lips unconsciously quirk up into a smile.

"Oh yes, and please include me in future discussions like the ones you two frequently had in the past," Carol requested politely, her tone of voice rather friendly. "I love reading books as well."

Anna happily accepted.

At that moment, however, Dylan returned to her side and suddenly took the glass of champagne from her hand. "No, you can't drink this. Are you planning on falling asleep in some random place again?"

David and Carol both wore intrigued expressions on their faces as if they hadn't expected Dylan to be so enamored as to fuss and dote over Anna like this.

"Come on," Anna protested. "I can handle at least this much."

"Well, I said you can't."

As the two bickered back and forth, a place full of delicious food suddenly presented itself before them. "If you can't drink, then have lots of food instead. It's all prepared for you, after all," Sir Crane, famous for being a gruff person, said to Anna. He wore an awkward look on his face.

Anna, genuinely happy, received the dish Sir Crane offered with relish. Along with it being a sign that he was welcoming her into the household, it was a means of conveying his remorse to Dylan. It was an apology. Dylan's eyes locked with his father's and he bowed his head, genuinely thanking

Sir Crane for the gesture.

"Thank you for the meal."

Anna lifted up one of the small pieces of finger food and was about to guide a mini pie with a strawberry on top of it between her plump lips when...

"*Mmf!*"

Without warning, she started to retch. The moment she smelled the food, she felt bloated and fought back the urge to vomit. She quickly handed Dylan the plate and covered her mouth and nose with her hands.

"What is it? Are you not feeling well?"

"Is it because she was feeling too nervous? Should I bring some cold water?"

Madam Jane, the only one who had been apart from the group, took this moment to join them, rushing to Anna's side and holding one of Anna's cold hands between hers. "Does the food smell that terrible?" she asked.

"I'm sorry, we're in a party all of you prepared for us, but I—" *hurk*! She heaved.

"No, it's fine," Madam Jane promised. Tears began to fall from her eyes. "I'm the one that's sorry."

"Mother? Are you crying right now?"

"Why are you suddenly crying, dear?"

Anna, despite being the only one who couldn't stop retching, felt worried about Madam Jane after seeing her cry.

At last, everyone in the Kilner family had finally come together in one place. All the hatred and jealousy they had for each other in the past must've